I0662206

THE REDSPEAR TEAM

BY

RON IDDON

LIFE IN A QUEENSLAND COUNTRY TOWN

*

A FICTION

Copyright (c) 2013 Ron Iddon (The Author)

"The Redspear Team" is a work of fiction; any resemblance between characters in the book and persons living or dead is accidental and unintentional.

The right of Ron Iddon to be identified as the author of this work has been asserted in accordance with the Copyright Amendment (Moral Rights) Act 2000.

All rights reserved. Without limiting the rights under the copyright reserved above, no part of this publication may be reproduced, stored in a retrieval system, or transmitted in any form or by any means, electronic, mechanical or photocopying, recording or otherwise, or used for any commercial purposes, without the prior written permission of the author.

Published by Leopardwood Productions, P. O. Box 4818, Toowoomba East, Queensland, 4350, Australia

Iddon, Ron 1940 –

The Redspear Team

ISBN 978-646-90299-9

Life in an inland Queensland town

Book design by Steven Wilson of Cranbrook Press, Toowoomba, Queensland, Australia

Type-set inTrajan Pro and Palatino, 9-22pt

Printed and bound by Lulu.com

A DROLL TALE.....

in which the author admits to a miscalculation.

***

I have had reason recently to recall that description once given of the *camel* – "a horse designed by a committee"; 'Redspear' is my camel.

When I at last settled down to beginning work on this **portrait of life in an Australian country town**, I had what I thought was the clever idea of using one of my characters from an earlier work.

Readers of "The Short Stories of Ron Iddon – The Queensland Collection" will remember **Hugh Watson**. He lived in such a town – **Redspear** – was a well educated man, observant, and a friend of many of that town's most interesting people. He 'contributed' several stories to 'Queensland'.

I now commissioned Hugh to put together "The Redspear Collection"; while he was to be free to write about his town and his friends as he chose, I made it clear – I *thought* I made it clear – that the manuscript should consist of short stories, *capable of being read in any order* – as is the custom with collections.

As all fiction writers know, our characters can be contrary, and this one was no different. Hugh began to *link* his stories, placing a development in one that would have consequences – consequences that would need to be dealt with in a later. I could see that, unchecked, this would mean that his stories would really only make sense if read in the order as presented. In effect, Hugh was converting *stories* into *chapters*; *my collection* was at risk of becoming *his novel*.

I remonstrated of course, but he was obdurate; I considered taking the project from him, but my problem there was that I liked what my alter ego was writing. I vacillated – eventually it was too late to act – and Hugh had won the day.

I dropped the word 'collection' from the book's title – yet "The Redspear *Team*" is not, in my opinion, a real novel; there is too little plot – and many of the 'chapters', with just a little tweaking, could still make stand alone stories.

So here we have my camel – though I have to say that of late I have been feeling more relaxed about that animal. Odd-looking yes, but it undoubtedly functions and survives, and I'm beginning to hope now, inspired by comments from those who have read the manuscript, that this member of the species might function and survive too.

RON IDDON

ACKNOWLEDGEMENTS AND THANKS

........to my editor, Letitia Gregory of Melbourne, who gave thoughtful and caring attention to every page and paragraph and line.

.......to Paul McNally of Toowoomba, whose reviewing of the manuscript helped me apply a final polish.

........and to all those friends and family members who provided kind words of encouragement during the gestation of 'Redspear'.

***

The original artwork for the front cover, showing Mary Carmody in the gazebo on the tower above her hotel, was created by Pat Freestone of Toowoomba.

RON IDDON

A WORD FROM THE PUBLISHERS

We convinced the author that several of the stories that appeared in his earlier book, "The Queensland Collection", also had a place in 'Redspear'.

"Liz and Me", "Like Errol", "Maggie" and "A Good Day's Work" now have second lives here.

 LEOPARDWOOD PRODUCTIONS

CONTENTS

ONE

LIZ AND ME

It was a hot afternoon on "Bull Run" and I'd come up from the cattle yards to have a drink and a rest. Liz was ironing some of the kids' clothes in the lounge room and I lay down on the floorboards nearby. She was barefooted, and whenever an ankle came within reach I massaged it, something she loved.

She stopped ironing. "When did you first realise you fancied me?"

"*Fancied* you?"

"You know, what – attracted you?"

My hand crept out but ankles stayed out of reach. "Everything."

She thumped a foot. " Hugh!"

"Do you mean – *the* moment?"

"Yes."

***

I certainly was not immediately attracted to Liz. On my early visits to Bull Run she had registered with me as just a tomboy, a dusty worker hardly distinguishable from her father's stockmen. Added

1

to that she was ten centimetres taller than yours truly, and I had never been attracted to tall girls.

I was twenty-three years of age and had just come up from the south. Two years before this I had graduated from Melbourne University, in Agricultural Economics, and had taken a job with one of the big pastoral agencies in that state. I was happy enough in my work, giving advice to agency clients, but then I read an advertisement by a group of Central Queensland graziers; they wanted someone to help them get better returns from their properties.

I liked the thought of it – big places and big operations; it would be an adventure – *and* a job I thought I could handle. As it turned out, this whiz kid was to spend two years *taking in* more knowledge than he imparted – something about which his employers proved to be very tolerant.

Their properties were in the district that surrounded a town called Redspear. I set up house in the town itself but found I spent most of my time out on the places themselves, and particularly at Bull Run. This large station, a hundred kilometres north of the town, was owned by the chairman of the group, Jack Dunn. His dining room, with its enormous cedar table, became my second office; many of the group's meetings took place around that table.

***

Jack was a widower, his wife having been killed in a driving accident many years before. He ran the property now with Liz, his only child, and she always sat in on any of the group's meetings.

Liz didn't say much at these times, perhaps just asking a question or two, and I have to say she did not at first make much of an impression on me. I guess I was full of the challenge of the new job. Probably full of myself too. Initially I thought she was only eighteen or nineteen, when she was actually twenty-two.

Her face would eventually become the dearest and most beautiful thing in the world to me, but even after several months I would have been unable to describe the colour of her eyes – even what her face *actually looked like*. She and I would sit across from each other at that table, yet had I ever really looked at those calm features, and into those hazel pools?

Later I would realise that Liz did not often look anyone full in the face, and when I mentioned this she said it was because she felt that when she did so it only reminded people of her height. "I was always tall – even at school. I was taller than all the boys."

Apparently it had become a habit, this looking off to one side during a conversation, and even with people taller than herself. After we talked about it though she dropped the habit, and almost overnight.

***

If our meetings at the Run went on late into the night I would sleep there, and if I had no appointments the next day I would help out with whatever was happening there. If the Dunns had cattle in the yards I would pitch into drafting or dipping or whatever, or I would ride out with the others if there was mustering to be done. If I may say so myself, I was able to make myself pretty useful, courtesy of skills I'd learned as a boy.

I began to be very impressed with Liz's abilities. She was a bold rider; she could estimate accurately the weight of a bullock; she could recite the pedigree of a bull; she could spot a conformation fault in a cow before anyone else.

I began to *like* her too – and she seemed to like me. She made this southern 'know-all' feel welcome.

***

3

At that time there were five stockmen employed on Bull Run plus a cook/housekeeper and her husband, the gardener/handyman. The staff ate in a room attached to the kitchen, which was separated from the homestead by a covered walkway. The owners and any guests were supposed to eat in the house itself, in that big dining room, but most of the time there were only Jack and Elizabeth there and they preferred to eat out with the staff.

Jack did not take the seat at the head of the table, and in fact he avoided it. He had initiated the custom of putting the newest stockman in it. Early in his occupancy of the chair, and when Jack thought he was ready, the newcomer was asked to tell everyone about his earlier life. This created some fun and at times perhaps some embarrassment for the new chum but it certainly broke the ice. Jack waited only two nights before he asked me to tell my story.

The men, and Deb the cook, all called Jack 'Mister' but that was the limit of any formality. He seemed to relish dinner times, and as soon as talk about local affairs flagged would bring up topics of national and international news. He challenged anyone who made a sweeping statement; it did not take a newcomer long to realise that a loose opinion would be pounced upon – but it all made for a lively time.

I was spending mealtimes at tables in homesteads all through the district at that time but none were more interesting or stimulating than those in the 'outside' room at Bull Run.

***

One afternoon, about nine months after I had taken up the job, I was going over some cash flow sheets on the dining room table when Jack called me out onto the back verandah. Across the flat below the homestead a single rider was leading a mob of perhaps three hundred prime bullocks. They were walking slowly, and the late sun was setting their shiny red coats afire. A blue cattle dog was bringing up the rear. The rider, on a white horse, was Liz.

"Nice sight," said Jack, somewhere between a statement and a question. I nodded, but I was looking only at Liz – so competent and so calm; something went click inside me.

***

"That!? Me on a horse!?"

"It was a very nice horse – Dillon I think."

"Duke."

"And they were beautiful Santas."

" Droughties."

"See?" I stretched out my arm. "I wasn't really looking at them."

Liz snorted and resumed ironing, but after a while began humming one of the old hymns she liked. An ankle came within reach, and stayed.

***

At breakfast the next morning Liz asked "well, don't you want to know?"

"Okay – when?"

Silence. I raised my eyebrows and she blushed.

"C'mon...."

"Alright." She gathered herself. "That night you were sitting at the head of the table and we asked you about your home down south."

"Why? What did I say?"

"You made it sound so nice. All your brothers. Your Mum and Dad. A real family."

"It wasn't always nice."

"I suppose. But it seemed nice to me. Anyhow, it made *you* nice." I got a kiss.

***

When I was growing up we lived in a town in the west of Victoria and my father was a senior employee of a big livestock agency. There was a takeover by another company and the new owners offered Dad the local managership. It would have meant a big increase in salary but he decided instead to start his own agency. *Their* agency: it would have been very much a joint decision between Mother and Dad.

We four boys had always been involved in Dad's work, even when we were little, helping him load and unload sheep and cattle at the saleyards, and penning up and keeping tallies; when the family struck out on its own we all became even busier, but we were older and I suppose more useful by then.

My own children would eventually help out on Bull Run in the same way, but more willingly I think. I and my brothers were always handling someone else's livestock but on the Run these were their own horses they saddled and their own cattle they rounded up and I'm sure that made a difference. I remember being not at all keen to get up at six on a southern winter's morning to go to the local saleyards and unload someone's fat lambs, but at the Run, if we had an early muster, there would be our bunch out on the verandah at dawn, tucking shirts into jeans and pulling on their elastic sided boots. Stumbling and still half asleep. Liz and I would stand at the kitchen door and watch the performance.

***

Dad used to give each of us a lot of responsibility yet I don't remember getting many *instructions* from him. And not much 'fathering' – moral guidance, that kind of thing. I think that when one is the youngest of four boys that sort of thing probably gets done quite capably by one's brothers.

Mother was different. She was a stickler for 'manners', and we were frequently given instructions in that department. Katherine's father had been a bank manager, and at that time – in that town – his family would have been considered 'society'. Katherine went to boarding school, and often stayed during holidays with school friends on their properties, in homesteads that were and are some of the grandest in the country.

It seemed to us boys that our speech and our manners were always being corrected by her – but perhaps our mixing with the stockmen at the saleyards made that necessary. We were always being told that something was "not a suitable expression." When I think back, Mother must have heard an awful lot that was 'unsuitable', but I don't seem to remember her becoming either shocked or angry. She always spoke politely to us, and in that special Western districts accent which is so distinct and familiar that I can still pick it today. Dad didn't speak with the accent, which is strange because he mixed a lot with people who did; perhaps the sons of grocers just did not speak that way.

Would you believe Mother used to leave *calling cards,* and we had a little silver dish on a table in the front hall for other people's cards (not that many left them). She also preserved the custom of not answering the front door herself; only if there were absolutely no other people in the house at all would Mother go to the door. She might not have been 'at home' you see.

When she did meet people however, she always asked after their families. She was *so* interested that they eventually told her about their more distant relatives as well, uncles and cousins and the like, and about anything and everything that was happening in their part of the country, *and she seemed to remember it all.* In later years district writers and historians were always phoning or visiting her;

if she did not know something about some person or event she was usually able to refer them to someone who did.

Later I urged her to put her recollections on paper or at least on tape, but it did not happen. I should have gone down and seen to it myself; when she died the Western Districts of Victoria lost an encyclopaedia.

Anyhow, as I was saying, there was this level of formality in our upbringing. We used to whinge about the lessons in manners, but of course bits stuck. Later I realised they actually had a practical value. Apart from anything else, they do allow one to screen or deter without causing embarrassment. As I remember Mother once saying, "you can laugh about dance cards, but I was able to shake off more than one unsuitable beau with a 'full' card."

***

Liz and I had finished breakfast and there were many things to do, for both of us, but we were dawdling. I caught her looking at me.

"What?"

That sweet smile. "Your mother."

"Yes?"

"She asked me once how you courted me."

I laughed: she did too.

***

We'd mustered a mob of heifers and were poking home in the late afternoon on a couple of tired horses. I had closed the last gate but hadn't yet remounted. We were talking, and I was leaning against her horse's neck. Liz's hand was resting on its wither right beside my face and I kissed it. She leaned down and kissed me on the lips. And that was it really – engaged.

TWO

JUST ME

I live in town now – have done for over twenty years. I still own "Bull Run", but I have also become an 'entrepreneur' in Redspear too; I own a very busy agricultural agency, and the local "Gazette", and am half-owner of a motel here. All three businesses are thriving. Four: 'Bull Run' is doing well too, managed for the last five years by one of my sons.

***

I moved to town after my darling Liz died – of breast cancer – at just forty. I won't dwell on the awfulness of that – her slow deterioration, and the devastation her death wrought amongst our family. I can sum it up by saying that I found I could not continue to live at the Run – there were just too many reminders of our happy life together – in the house, in the homestead surrounds – even out on the station itself. In a way I think I was going a little bit mad then; I would often fancy that I could still hear her singing. She loved to sing.

I put on a manager, moved the hundred kilometres or so into Redspear and began a new life. The three older children were attending boarding school in Brisbane at that time but I brought our youngest with me into town.

***

I borrowed against the Run, bought this house – and immediately found I became very busy, and in an unexpected way. Friends decided that because I now must have plenty of time on my hands they would ask me to seek out particular pieces of machinery for them, or to track down lines of cattle. They said the established agencies in town were hopeless at it – weren't really interested.

I realised I was doing what my father used to do with his agency in western Victoria. Dad would often talk to us boys about his clients and what they wanted. "None of you knows someone with an old Commer do you?" he might ask – and quite often we did. Mother would help out if she could see we were stymied, and *she'd* talk to someone. That kind of thing was very effective.

I made a very big decision; I decided there was room in Redspear for an agency that gave this old-fashioned service. I bought a two hectare block on the edge of town, set up a couple of demountables on it, and began "Watson and Co". I wanted a really keen and well qualified person to help me, and advertised nationally. I received such good applications that I put on not one but two young men.

***

We lost money for the first year – as I more or less expected we would – but by the end of the second year we began to move into the black. This would actually have happened sooner but for the fact that many of my clients expected *credit*, and for fairly long periods.

I hadn't realised how prevalent this practice was; eventually I was carrying several hundred thousand dollars of delayed payments but still I was losing customers to the big boys like Elders and Dalgety's, because I couldn't match their credit facilities.

I introduce now the third of the triumvirate of those women who have had the most influence on my life, Mary Carmody. She was – and still is – the owner of our largest hotel – a spinster, going on seventy at that time, and rich – moderately so at the time but astoundingly so today.

A direct but friendly woman, and someone I already knew quite well, she rang one day and invited me to her hotel for afternoon tea and a talk. This took place in her luxurious first floor apartment there, with best china and salmon sandwiches, brought by one of the housemaids. I wondered what was coming, but had to wait for the second cup before she broached the reason for the invitation.

"You are happy with the way the agency is developing?"

"Yes I think so."

"It's not easy to make a success of a new business."

"You certainly have to do your homework." I was a little guarded; she could well have been thinking of competing.

She read my mind. "Relax Hugh. I am not a threat to your new business. Possibly quite the opposite." She revealed that she knew about the demands on me for credit, as of course she would; she knew and still knows everything that happens in Redspear.

She put the proposition that she *act as bank* to Watson and Co, allowing me to draw on her funds to accommodate my clients. She would charge one percent more than solicitor mortgage rates and she wanted to be allowed to check each agreement.

"I know some of the local gentry perhaps a little better than you Hugh."

It was good news, and when she told me the extent of the funds she could commit, it was bloody great news. I knew I would be able to handle virtually every client who came to me; the only real bar to full competition with the big agencies was about to be removed. She ordered champagne; it was French of course.

***

A year later she asked if I might be interested in joining her in buying the Sunset Motel. This is a budget affair on the western edge of town; it was a bit run down then and I was not much enthused at first but changed my attitude after I had gone through the figures.

"These are good, and I think we could even improve on them. Why don't you buy it outright?" She merely shrugged, and I did not pursue it – after all I was being offered what looked like a good proposition; over the years I have come to think that she may have proposed the partnership simply because she felt like it. Perhaps, after so many years as a 'sole trader', she liked the idea of doing something in tandem.

***

Five years after this I was offered "The Gazette". I was at the front desk placing an ad one day when the owner and editor Phil Owens asked me to come into his office and, out of the blue, asked me if I would be interested.

"But I know nothing about newspapers Phil," I protested. "It's always seemed to me such a complicated business." Whenever I and my youngest son Nicholas had wandered through the backrooms of the Gazette, and they were preparing an edition, I had found it an incomprehensible process.

"Hugh, it's a *business*. And you understand business."

"But the – technical stuff......?"

"You leave that to Kent."

And who was Kent? His nephew, who was a trained printer and who was already running a country newspaper in southern N.S.W.; he wanted to move north.

"He's good, Hugh. A worker. And smart." And that has proven to be true.

***

So today Hugh Watson is the proprietor of a cattle station and a newspaper and a farm agency and half a motel – sixty-three, very healthy, a widower, father of four and grandfather of six.

Ralph, my second son, does a very good job out at the Run, as I said. Bill, my eldest, is in city real estate – in Melbourne now – and Julie is married and living on her husband's family's property about halfway between here and Brisbane, a very handy overnight stop for her old dad when he drives to that city.

***

My youngest, Nicholas, was just three years of age when we moved to Redspear. When he was old enough to go to boarding school, as the others had done, I decided against sending him. My other children, particularly Bill, argued that he *had* to go, for the broader education, the valuable contacts – the usual reasons – but frankly I just could not stand to lose the last of the children – my last link with Liz.

I decided I could do a good job of it here. I had always believed it is the atmosphere at home that determines whether a child does well at his schooling and I gave it my best – reading to him when he was young, taking an interest in his school work, encouraging him – all that. And we *talked* a lot – about his friends, the future – even world affairs – everything. He accompanied me whenever it was possible, not just on social visits but business too; I never excluded him.

By the time he went to university in Brisbane he was so relaxed in every circumstance, so adaptable – such a good mixer – that I think, if I may say so, I *had* done a good job. He did well at uni too, and has a good position now in Brisbane as a graphics designer.

***

But – it is just me in this house here now. I do talk frequently on the phone to my offspring, and I meet a lot of people at the agency and the motel and the newspaper – and I have a good social life generally – but, at the end of the day – most days – I am here in this house on my own.

It's a nice house – only a fraction of the size of the old homestead on Bull Run but big enough for me. Like many older houses in Redspear it has open verandahs all round, and in the northeast corner of those verandahs I have set up a little table and a couple of those low slung deck chairs with extending leg supports that we call "squatters".

It is here, with a whisky bottle and glass on the table and my two dogs lying on the boards, one on either side of me, that I read and write in the late afternoon. I like the feel and sounds of my town at this time of day – awaiting, as an old Scottish woman once said to me, the "fall of the night". I hear women calling their children in – the ringing of bicycle bells – the kids' last shouts – laughter – and cars going slowly home.

 I do regret of course that there will be no-one else in the house with me during the night – someone I love and who loves me; we are meant to live in families aren't we. And what makes me feel this lack most strongly at this time is the sound of a woman singing.

This corner of the house is close to my neighbours' kitchen and Geraldine sings while she prepares the evening meal for Don and their two little kids. For some reason this young woman likes the songs of the Thirties and Forties, as Liz did and as I do now, and the hymns from Sunday School days. I hum along, and even sing

– quietly: secret duets. It takes me back to those wonderful days at Bull Run. I don't feel sad – well, sometimes a bit – but you must not feel sorry for me; I have 'moved on', as they say, and know I have in fact a very fortunate life.

If Geraldine's kitchen window were not open I would scarcely hear her; she has a nice voice, but small, and I doubt if anyone else outside her family can hear. Just me.

THREE

TREASURES

I love early Australian buildings. Whenever I drive through a country town that I haven't visited before, I take notice of them; often I stop and get out of the vehicle for a closer look, and I always read any plaque or board that the locals have put up.

Those buildings can tell one so much about the history of a town. I think of those grand hotels and public offices in towns like Bendigo and Ballarat: gold! By contrast the tiny corrugated iron houses in the back streets of Broken Hill – many of them moved there from worked-out mines elsewhere – speak quietly to me of the hard scrabble life back then. And that lavish use of what we regard today as valuable cabinet timbers in the ordinary joists and beams of the first houses in the towns in eastern Queensland surely reaffirms just how heavily timbered that land must have been when first colonised.

In Redspear our old houses are typical of most early homes in towns throughout western Queensland, which by and large were built to cope with the long hot summers – high ceilings, fairly steep roofs and verandahs (sometimes on all four sides, and often with French doors opening onto them) – and raised off the ground on stumps, some just a metre or so but many two and three metres.

Of our larger buildings we have two that the National Trust has listed – "fundamental to the history and character of Redspear" I think the wording goes – the convent and the railway station.

The convent is wide and double storeyed, and of classic Georgian design, but to which verandahs were added, at the front and sides. It was the first building in our town to be made of brick – a soft salmon colour; there are French doors and lots of cast iron lace.

Sometime in its history, in the 1920's I have been told, a decision was made to erect screens of lattice along the verandahs, possibly to give the nuns more privacy. At the moment they are painted white and in the early morning sunlight they are quite dazzling. Because the nuns no longer live in it, we debated at a Trust meeting recently whether to remove the screens but we decided to leave them because we reckoned they had been there so long that they were part of its history too. I would soften them a bit if I had my way – paint them cream perhaps.

Our railway station was built in 1895, in timber, and in high Victorian style – all turrets and flourishes. It is not a tall building but of course quite long. For decades it was painted in basic Government cream and brown, and then we had Heritage ox blood with dark green. It is now mulberry and white, which some might say makes it look like a decorated cake; I think it looks great.

There is another building that I think is 'fundamental to the character and history' of our town and that is Carmody's Hotel. It is in the main street, in brick, on the site of the original timber one that was destroyed in a fire during the Second World War.

 I do not understand how Stan Carmody was able to put up such an enormous building at that time. Weren't there restrictions at the end of the War, on building supplies and materials, and didn't Governments make decisions about which projects could be approved? This one would have required *dozens* of builders and labourers and used enough bricks and iron and timber to make *fifty* houses.

Carmody's dominates our main street; it takes up a whole block and is two storeys high. It looks older than its sixty years because of the *style* the owner chose – something that I suppose one could call 'Post Federation' – corrugated iron on the roof and the awnings and verandahs, but not bull-nosed. It is not as 'pretty' as the colonial era buildings, and it is massive – eighty metre frontage to the main street, and again in both side streets.

The present owner, Stan's daughter Mary, added a tower on one main street corner in the 1980's – Redspear's new *red spear*. She had big windows put in it so she could look out over the town when she went up into it. This was, some might say, a fairly extravagant thing to do but if you knew the lady you would know it was quite in character. And a few years later Mary gave some of our builders a new challenge – to raise the roof of the tower and leave an open space beneath it – to make a sort of gazebo in the sky. Until our new television mast was installed Mary's tower was the highest thing in town; one can see it from ten kilometres away.

***

There is one treasure here that is not architectural and which nearly all visitors have heard about before arriving, and are very keen to see – our icon.

***

When the first white men arrived at this reach of the Ferguson River in the mid-1800's, and decided to make permanent camp on the big waterhole here while they reconnoitred to the west for land to take up, they saw an Aboriginal spear leaning against one of the coolabahs near the water's edge. It was unusually long and heavy, and coated in red ochre.

Our town developed around that tree and its spear – and by the way a town that called itself in those early years *Red Spear* but through some bureaucratic bungling or interference in Brisbane came to be listed officially as we know it today.

When the town site was moved to the western bank of the river, because the sandy soil here was more stable for building on, the spear was brought over too. About this time a visiting anthropologist tried to take it back to Brisbane's Museum but the locals refused to release it. I am glad they did.

Today the spear is housed in our Civic Centre, upright in an impressive timber and glass case.

***

When the Sesquicentenary Celebrations were held, it was taken out of its case and placed once more against the coolabah, which is still alive. A late afternoon ceremony was held there depicting the arrival of that first party of would-be squatters. Some copies of taped early recordings of corroboree were played, sent up from the Brisbane Museum.

That evening of the re-enactment I noticed how the red ochre of the spear caught the last rays of the setting sun – it seemed to *flame* – and in the night it again picked up light from the settlers' campfire. I found my eye was repeatedly drawn to the spear.

We were celebrating the first white settlement of this region – newcomers claiming the land – but it didn't take much imagination to feel that the spear was silently repeating a much older claim.

***

No-one has ever determined the identity of the man who left the spear. I have read some notes in our Library from one of the early residents who tried to find out from the older Aborigines, but even they had been unable to shed any light on his identity. There was agreement though that he must have been tall and strong. How interesting it would have been to hear *his* story.

FOUR

MARY

Carmody's Hotel has a special place in my own story; it was my first home here.

***

I arrived at the end of my drive from Victoria in January 1972. There was no-one in the main street, absolutely no-one. My impression, when I drove my Holden utility across the rattley little wooden bridge over the Ferguson, was of coming onto an unused movie set. If I were doing the shooting script I might have written – "Redspear, a smallish town on the mid-western plains of Queensland. It is a hot Sunday afternoon in Summer. There are no people to be seen on the streets; a pair of crows circle slowly above the main street, and the only sound is that of their mournful cries."

I drove past the front of the two-storey hotel and around the corner into its back yard, which was still unpaved at that time. There were several doors on the ground floor, closed and, I found, all locked. After I parked the ute I walked around to the main street again to try the front entrance.

It was dark inside the foyer, which was the full two storeys high. There was a giant but unlit chandelier; later I would learn that Sunday afternoons were the only times it was turned off. Sometimes now, forty years later, I take visitors to the hotel to see that same chandelier in full blaze.

It was very quiet but after a while I realised I could hear voices, low and muffled. It was a conversation, between I thought a man and a woman, but I couldn't locate them; they seemed to be behind a wall. I thought I'd stay where I was – someone was bound to come through soon. I sat on a lounge at one side of that foyer. It too reminded me of a film set: "Enter butler left".

What did enter was Wolfie, the biggest dog I had ever seen. He came out of the gloom near the back of the stairs and walked straight towards me. I would later learn that he was the most mild tempered of dogs but right then he terrified me; he was obviously a guard dog and I felt at that moment like an intruder. He stopped right in the centre of the room and looked at me. After a minute I got up enough nerve to speak to him: "nice doggie", that kind of thing. No response. He just stood there, which I found even more menacing than if he had growled. I kept talking to him, with my voice becoming more and more choked. Would nobody come? I called again but no-one answered. At last the dog turned and walked up the stairs, to my very great relief.

After a while I realised that the voices were coming from a radio. Then they stopped and I heard footsteps and one of the side doors opened. A young woman greeted me and said the owner was having a rest but that she'd left instructions that I was to be shown to my room.

I was taken up the stairs and along one wide hallway then down another. The enormous building would become very familiar to me eventually but that first day it was a maze, and even a bit forbidding. Shirley said that Mary would see me at six o'clock in her office downstairs. How would I find that, I wondered?

Do you remember how the bedrooms in big old country hotels were – dark paint and heavy furniture? The curtains in mine were closed so it was gloomy: no air conditioning of course. When my guide left it was as quiet as the grave. I unpacked and went off to find the bathroom, which was on a monumental scale too, and when I came back I lay down on sheets which I noticed had been ironed – -Mother had always had our sheets ironed; I immediately nodded off.

I woke about five and found my way round to the car to get my bags. It was still baking hot in that yard and it took me about four trips to bring in all my stuff. I still did not see anyone; it was as if the housemaid and the dog and myself were the only living things in Redspear.

I was a healthy and confident young man but that afternoon quite took the edge off my spirits.

***

I lived at Carmody's for several months and very soon made myself at home. I learned that Sunday afternoons were the only times the hotel was quiet; the rest of the time the building teemed with people—in the bars and the lounges and the dining rooms.

My new job as advisor to a group of graziers meant I had to travel all over the district, and I came and went at all hours. The owner Mary gave me my own key, which opened one of the doors onto the rear courtyard. I used to cook myself some eggs or a steak late at night in the vast kitchen, and help myself to puddings from the equally vast cool rooms. Wolfie and I became pals.

***

Mary had inherited the hotel from her father, when she was thirty. She was now in her late forties – unmarried – a tall woman, broad shouldered and handsome. Handsome if one looked only at the side of her face that had not been badly burned, in the fire that had destroyed the original timber hotel – and killed her mother, who was the housekeeper/manager. Mary had been only twenty then.

Once I had overcome my initial and no doubt immature reactions to her disfigurement I very much enjoyed our conversations, which usually took place late at night. She asked me all about my family and my upbringing in Victoria. She asked me about Melbourne, which she had never visited.

She also had a great curiosity about the lives of the people in her own part of the world, and because I got about such a lot, I was grilled at length. She wanted all the gossip, though to my knowledge she never repeated it. And she has not changed – she still wants all the details. And still gives advice. Freely.

She used to tell me about her plans to renovate the hotel – and other business ideas she had – and even ask my opinions, which was flattering. Perhaps it was because I was an outsider.

***

Today, forty years on, I visit the place at least once a week, to join friends at the bar, have a meal or just to impress any visitors I may have. If I can, I arrange for them to meet Mary.

Over the years the old girl has made her hotel the centre of social and – really – *commercial* activity in Redspear, activity that has increased probably tenfold since I arrived in the early 70's, with the building of the dam on the Ferguson and the coming of irrigation. Many business deals have been initiated in those bars or lounges or in the dining room.

I really must make more of an effort to get across the *scale* of Carmody's. It is far bigger than any hotel I know of in central Queensland, even those I have visited on the coast. And with that size there is *style*, courtesy of the lady's tastes (and income, which, I happen to know, is abundant.)

Take the big dining room. Mary has had it done in French *fin de siécle* style, with lots of paintings and gilt mirrors and lighting from what looks like a hundred wall sconces with gold shades. There's a burgundy carpet and heavy cream napery over the many large round tables.

Dining at Mary's tends to take on a festive character and can end up being very expensive. One might go there with a group of friends *intending* to have just the basic meal, which one would have to say is still largely 'country'; in winter it's soups and roasts, or perhaps grills and hotpots, and the kinds of desserts that city restaurants no longer serve, like Queen pudding, bread and butter pudding and fruit pies, with custard and cream. In summer there are consommés and salads and seafood and chicken, but grills too, and jellies and trifles and fruits and ice cream.

It's a set dinner at a set price but things do tend to get out of hand. A lot of drinking can take place, especially if Mary herself joins the party, and it's generally not your average wine but the good stuff, and champagne, and brandy and port – though to be fair Mary buys more than her share. After thinking that you will be home by 9.30 you find you're still going strong at midnight. No-one seems to regret it though.

***

Mary's own apartment is on the main street, next to the corner, up on the first floor. At some stage she had several interior walls removed, to give herself one huge living room. In the 1980's she had it redecorated, and it is something to see.

The windows have heavy cream silk drapes. The ceiling, which is at least four and a half metres high, is a dark green, the walls emerald. The end wall is all books, to the ceiling, with one of those library ladders on castors. Throughout the room antique furniture glows under a chandelier that I know takes someone half a day to polish. The carpet is wool, soft and thick, champagne coloured with a subtle pattern. Think of a formal drawing room in an English 'stately home'.

There's a carved rosewood screen and behind it a television set and a DVD player. The speakers are virtually invisible, fitted into the corners of the room. There's an ornate cast iron spiral staircase in the corner, rescued by Mary from a public library in Brisbane that was being demolished; it leads to a door that opens into her tower.

If one were the kind of person who feels ill at ease in luxurious surroundings one would most definitely feel that way here. That same person could also be somewhat daunted by the woman herself. She is tall, and always wears shoes with some heel. Stockings, of course, and what I think women would call "frocks", to the mid calf. Top frocks too, if I am any judge. And spectacular jewellery that you know is the real thing. As I may have said, this woman is very rich.

Whatever she may have felt in the early days about her facial disfigurement – from the fire – she makes few concessions to it now. She does affect a hairstyle that holds her hair close to her face, and at race meetings and the like I have seen her wear a little hat with a veil, but otherwise she seems to have adopted the attitude that people just have to accept her disfigurement.

She is nearly ninety now, but carries herself as I think she has always done – head up, wide shoulders back – no slouching. To see Mary leaving the hotel in full regalia puts one in mind of the Queen Mary leaving Southampton; one can almost hear the tugs.

**

She and I are having a late afternoon drink in her apartment when we are interrupted by a loud "aark". Mary goes to the little refrigerator behind the wooden panelling and takes out a small parcel of chopped meat. "Aark". I follow her to the spiral staircase and up into the tower and out onto the gazebo.

Her visitor sits on a rail on the eastern side. I stand back while Mary walks towards the glossy black bird, pulling a small piece of meat from the package. She puts it down on the rail and the bird takes four or five paces, picks it up and swallows it. Mary comes back to me and puts another piece down on the rail beside us. The crow walks towards us along the rail with that rolling gait birds have, seeming to look at me all the time but not stopping. This piece of meat is longer and he tries to break it up by flicking it with his beak against the rail. He does not succeed, and after fifteen seconds he raises his beak and swallows it whole.

"He won't take it from my hand. He has tremendous patience. It's willpower really. He *wills* me to put it down. Even if I put it on the palm of my hand right under his nose he won't take it. Watch." And she holds her hand just in front of the bird with a piece of glistening red beef on it. The bird does not touch it, seeming to look anywhere but at the meat. "He's a tough old bird. Or she."

Which makes two of them. Formidable. One with a heart though. One who has given, I would estimate, two million dollars to worthy causes in the past thirty years. And who has been a very good friend to me, one I treasure, even if I do have to submit to her questions about every detail of my life.

"Look, there's Helen" and she points to a mutual friend down in the main street. We watch as the younger woman approaches the street awnings and disappears under them.

"You've known her almost as long as you've known me."

"Early eighties," she corrects, "but yes, she's a good friend." For some reason she adds, "But you know Hugh we've never become … intimate. There's always a little reserve there."

"You mean Helen Carruthers doesn't tell you everything about her daily life?"

"No." Looking at me keenly.

"And you cannot pry?"

"No," clasping her hands now in front of her.

"And give advice on all matters business or personal?" She drops her head and nods.

"And in general intrude on each and every aspect of her life so that she – or any friend – can regard nothing as completely private?" She is gone now, rocking backwards and forwards, her shoulders shaking. Such compliments! What pleasure!

When she has pulled herself together and wiped her eyes she says, "I'm afraid I never hear such nice words from my other friends."

FIVE

HELEN

Mary would certainly never hear such words from the mutual friend we had just seen down in the street, Helen Carruthers. Helen is the manager and part-owner of "The Bauhinias", our town's upmarket motel; the other owner is Mary herself.

***

Helen is tall, slim and certifiably beautiful – short black hair and a face of film star quality. I am sure that when she turns those grey eyes onto a traveller, especially if it is a male, and adds a smile, any thought of driving further evaporates.

Though Helen must be almost fifty now she could easily pass for thirty-five. She is a divorcee, another fact that has triggered the attention of quite a few of Redspear's males, eligible and non-eligible – but she has remained unattached and, apparently, happily so.

***

She grew up in Brisbane and began her working life as a primary school teacher near there but soon felt unsuited to the job. She

31

looked for something different, and certainly got that when she replied to the advertisement Mary Carmody had placed in "Queensland Country Life" – someone to help rejuvenate the businesses which lined the street frontages under the awnings of the woman's hotel.

It is – or was – quite common to see shops sheltering under the awnings of big country hotels in this state, but in this case, back in the 1980's, the shops at Carmody's were not profitable. Only some were let, and the lessees were not paying much.

Helen had had no business experience at all, but the older woman trusted her instincts and took her on. Helen did a good job Mary has told me – and under quite a handicap; her employer did not want any of her tenants hurt. She agreed that the rents needed to be raised but she made it clear that none of the tenants were to be forced out if they could not afford more. Old Mary is tough in business, but she can be a softie too.

***

Helen began with the three empty shops. In the 80's there were still no proper 'Take-Aways' in the town; Helen set up one of the premises with ovens and fryers and advertised for a new lessee; that man – a couple actually – quickly found that Redspear's citizens were just like other Australians in their fondness for fish and chips, chickens and hamburgers. Helen asked for and got a rental figure twice that of the others. She also set up a mini supermarket and a shoe shop and had no trouble getting lessees for them also.

With the permission of the old lessees she renovated *their* stores and then began to nudge them into expanding their businesses. As they succeeded she was able to increase their rents too. Within eighteen months she had transformed Carmody's Corner.

***

Mary began to ask Helen to do extra things, like meeting VIPs, and arranging and even hostessing social functions in the hotel.

"She was very good Hugh," her former employer told me. "Very, very good. She had that touch of city confidence. A flair too. And of course she looked marvellous, especially when she dressed up. Actually I think she looks even better today. What was she then ... twenty-two, twenty-three? You must remember her then?"

I did. My wife and I had gone to several functions at the hotel at the time. Liz had told me the talk in the powder room was often about trying to keep husbands from making fools of themselves over Helen.

The partnership between Helen and Mary lasted only three years though before Helen Carruthers became Helen Platt, grazier's wife.

***

I did know the Platts at that time, but only slightly. They had a property well to the south of town and as Bull Run is a hundred kilometres to the north we did not meet that often – just at race meetings and that kind of thing. Gerald Platt had inherited "Sebastopol" from his parents and didn't marry Marjorie until rather late in life; they had had just the one child, John.

After John returned from boarding school he worked on the family place and also for other district landholders. He was good at cricket and rugby. I met him only the once back then – a tall and good looking young man with reddish blonde hair. I think he would have been in his late twenties when he married Helen.

The Platts set up the newlyweds on a new place to the west of Redspear and in short order there were two daughters. I did meet the good-looking young couple on and off over the next few years – but had no idea their marriage was crumbling.

***

Our town's appearance has changed a lot since I arrived here. The 'dry' look has long disappeared, thanks to the abundant water from the big dam on the Ferguson; now all of our streets are shaded by Leopard and Casuarina and Jacaranda trees. We citizens have gone mad with our gardens too; compared with the desiccated little town on the plains that I encountered in 1972 Redspear today is an oasis.

Even amongst this botanical splendour though Helen's motel on the river still stands out, because of the old Bauhinia trees that line the entrance; their flowers in winter – white, lilac and red – make a spectacular show.

If I am down at the river end of the main street and I have some spare time I drop in to The Bauhinias for a chat. These are never the 'everything on the table' talks that I am forced to have with Mary though; there *is* this touch of reserve about Helen. She rarely shares personal confidences.

Which is why I was surprised one day recently when she began to talk about her marriage. She had prepared drinks, a mix of rum, lime and water that we both like, and we had made our way down to a seat near the lagoon below her private quarters at the rear of the motel. Helen has made it very nice there, and the Council sometimes hires the spot for receptions and the like.

As usual Ernie, the resident black swan, walked up, stretched to his full height and width and flapped mightily; his admiring audience clapped and he ambled off. I told Helen about a swan that Liz used to have as a pet.

"Did you know Liz very well when you got married?" Out of the blue.

"Pretty well," I said.

"I really didn't know John." She paused. "I didn't realise that he wasn't used to making decisions." She paused again. "And he was bad with money Hugh. I think Marj and Gerald had always made all the financial decisions.

34

When we were on our own place he used to make impulsive purchases of cattle and machinery. I tried to get him to talk things over with me first but he wouldn't. Or couldn't.

It used to worry me; we had a big overdraft and I knew we had to be very careful with what we spent. Working with Mary had taught me about money. She would always *spend*, but only if she was satisfied it was justified. I really had to do my homework if I went to her with a proposition. John would hardly listen at all when I tried to talk about things like cash flows and budgets.

The Platts had borrowed against "Sebastopol" to get us onto "Farlyle" and we had big interest payments to make. Then that credit squeeze came in. It probably didn't worry the big places so much but it drove us under. Do you remember it?"

I certainly did; it had made things pretty sticky for us too for a couple of years.

"Mr. and Mrs. Platt got almost panicky about their bank repayments and that put a lot of pressure on us – it was really much worse than if we'd owed the money directly to the bank ourselves.

I don't know if it was this pressure or just... us, but our marriage couldn't hold up. It got that way we could scarcely have a conversation that didn't end in an argument.

John got a job at the Cheviot mine driving trucks and that was a big help, financially; you know the mines pay very well. But the girls and I didn't see him very much from then on. He used to stay at their quarters overnight and come home only every third day or so but sometimes he wouldn't be home for a week. He said he was doing extra shifts but he only seemed to be earning the same money. I think he just preferred staying out at the mine."

***

I knew Mary would have known all this, so I felt free to talk about it with her.

35

"Did she tell you anything else?"

"We were interrupted. She was wanted at the office."

Mary then told me of an incident that must have crushed whatever goodwill was remaining in their relationship.

"Helen went back to teaching here in town, two days a week. She and the two girls stayed overnight here. It was lovely to have her around – though it made me realise again what I had lost when she married John. Of course I knew about the strain between them; it was a real mis-match that one – should never have come about.

Besides the part-time teaching job, Helen had taken on the rearing of turkeys for the Christmas market. I think I must have mentioned how I always had trouble getting nice fresh birds at that time and she must have sounded out a few other people – shopkeepers and friends – and blow me down she orders all these turkey chicks – *three hundred* if memory serves. She told me that she'd learned they were easy to rear and since they already had a couple of big sheds with wire runs at Farlyle, and plenty of grain on hand, she thought she'd give it a try.

The Department man had offered to come out and check on them every now and then; he was a single man, nice fellow – I think he might have been a bit taken with Helen – but that wouldn't have been surprising.

One of the things Helen used to do was to let all of the birds out to free range when she could; she told me the girls kept an eye on them then like guard dogs. Pretty safe really, in the daytime – no foxes around then. Helen would leave them locked in their runs for the two days each week she was spending in town.

This time John was coming back to Farlyle on the Friday morning to wash some clothes and get some other things, and Helen asked him to fix a leak in the main house tank while he was there. He'd said that it would probably take a few hours to do that because he would first have to let the tank run dry and then fill it up afterwards, so she

36

asked him if he would let the turkeys out during that time, and put them back in again before he left. Apparently they always went back in easily.

Hugh – when she got home – there were dead turkeys everywhere – all around the homestead and down the paddock – even out on the road. It looked like they had been killed by dogs. There were only about fifty left alive.

Imagine that homecoming! And Helen thought immediately that John had done it – that he'd let his dogs loose on them. That's how bad things had become between them."

***

Mary said Helen rang her husband at the mine that night but they said he wasn't there. A few days later the manager phoned her to say he'd received a phone call from John saying he'd had to go away on urgent family business, and a week later there was a letter from him to the manager saying he wouldn't be back. It was postmarked Northern Territory.

Within six months Helen had handed Farlyle back to her parents-in-law and was living in Redspear, and teaching full-time once again. A year later she and John were divorced; Mary said she believes Helen never heard from the man again.

SIX

LIKE ERROL

My own motel does not compare with "The Bauhinias" – definitely more down-market. 'Clean, Comfortable, Affordable' is our motto at "The Sunset" – or, more correctly, that of Errol, my manager.

It's at the western end of our main street, and I call in there about once a week to talk things over with Errol. He's easy to find; I just have to switch the engine off and listen. If he's not talking with someone, joking and laughing – and he does have a carrying voice – he's *singing*. He favours the rock numbers of the 60's – Elvis, Bobby Darin, the Everly Brothers – all those.

I don't know what the customers think of him – although I suppose I do because they *keep returning*. I sometimes read the filled-in 'Invitation to Comment' forms the girls leave in the rooms. If there is a witty remark about his style – or his singing – he puts it up on the office wall. That's like Errol.

***

It was five years ago that Errol walked into the agency office and asked me for a job. He told me he'd grown up on a dairy on the coast, worked at the local milk factory and then moved up to

Manningham with his wife and got a job in a big hardware and farm supplies store. As he described it, his job there involved a bit of everything but mainly serving customers.

I know the store; it is huge, and looks a bit old-fashioned, but over the years it has built up a very good reputation, particularly for service. I happen to know through a business contact that its turnover is enormous.

I hadn't remembered seeing this solidly-built, energetic looking young man the last time I called there but now as he talked I could imagine him on the job there – racing around the counters, serving two customers at once and assuring another he would be just a minute – that sort of person. He told me he liked it there but it was a wage job with not enough incentive and he was looking for something more. He said he had always been interested in moving out west and, flatteringly, told me he had heard I ran a good business.

My profit depends on sales, and as it happened I *had* been thinking of putting on another salesman. Errol said if I took him on he would like to be paid on a straight commission basis – a mark I thought of his self-confidence. When I said that I would consider him I got a big grin and another vigorous handshake.

He'd come prepared, and gave me the names and phone numbers of two people as references; I always use my own sources though to check out possible employees, and within a day I had learned all I needed.

Because I know that it can be hard for a newcomer if he is depending only on commissions, I offered him a base salary as well – the same deal as my other employees had – and within a fortnight Errol was up and running.

***

I did wonder if I might have got hold of a tiger by the tail. An agricultural agency such as mine depends as much on personal relations and reputation as it does upon prices. A regular client will buy from us even if he can get whatever it is a bit cheaper somewhere else – and if we don't have what he wants he knows we will get it in for him. If he returns something that he says is faulty he can rely on us to replace it without question, or have it repaired. If he cannot pay for a few months he knows we will accommodate him.

What I was edgy about with Errol was that he might put 'the deal' above all else, just to earn that commission. I could imagine him guaranteeing delivery of something when we couldn't, or talking someone into buying something he really didn't need, or could afford. I took pains to get across to him that the *people* side of the business was the most important.

Well, I needn't have worried. He did increase our turnover – considerably – but for all his 'go' he was a people person too; I think people found that purchasing something through friendly Errol was just the natural end to a meeting with him.

There were times when he came back from visiting a farmer with an order so much bigger than we had ever had from that person that I felt sure we'd get a phone call changing it – but it didn't happen. Errol untied some of the district's tightest purse strings, and seemingly without effort.

***

His phone technique was a revelation. His calls sounded simply social – no hint of a 'sell'. Somehow it was the client himself who came up with the idea of buying something – or thought he did.

At a Field Day or the annual Show where we had our own tent and a display of machinery and implements he was unstoppable. He would make sure we had tables and folding chairs and sandwiches and tea and cold drinks, and once again what had all the appearance of a social get together delivered a lot of business.

***

You can imagine it was with mixed feelings that I learned after just two years with me he wanted to leave the agency and run the motel I had purchased. "But you're doing so well here!" I said. And so, as a consequence, was I. "You're earning twice as much as you were on the coast."

"I know but I'll be good for the motel. And you can find someone to do this. I'll help you find him."

"You like this job Errol. Let me find another Errol to run the motel."

"I've thought about it; it's what I'd really like to do." My face must have been a study because he said "I'll start off on an ordinary wage," but then, because this was Errol, "when I build it up though I'd like to share in that. More like partners."

Smiling – and so keen what could one do.

***

It turned out that Errol was perfect for Sunset. It took on a different look and atmosphere from the day he went there. He painted all the timberwork and made the entrance more attractive and renewed the lawns and put in more shrubs and trees. He put up a new sign and had "Under New Management" put on a board underneath. The place got a lot busier; we didn't increase our rates but the returns jumped.

He wanted to put our prices on a sandwich board at the driveway entrance but I was against that. I had always felt that if I saw such a sign outside a motel it was an indication that it wasn't doing well. Another thing was that I didn't want to enter a price war with the other motel in town.

42

"It won't happen," said Errol. "Helen Carruthers won't need to drop her prices. She shouldn't. It's a different clientele."

I argued my other point – about it making the place look a bit 'desperate'. Errol looked at me for a few seconds without saying anything, as if gathering his thoughts – unusual for him to do that.

"Well, I always look for that price board. I want to know before I drive in that I can afford it. I don't want to have to drive out again to go somewhere else."

It was a reminder to me of the difference in our financial situations, and how my wealth was cutting me off from the experiences of people like him. We did it his way.

***

Errol never collected his wife from Manningham. He said in the early days that he was waiting to get a suitable house. He used to drive down each weekend – but then these trips became less frequent. He began turning up at parties, and with local girls; he got the nickname 'Flynn' of course.

 The only concern I have ever had with Errol is over his love life, about which he is very enthusiastic. In the two years he was at the agency he had a variety of 'friends', around town and in the district. It seemed that they couldn't say no to him and he couldn't say no to them.

Rural Queensland is a conservative place and I thought Errol's activities might have harmed our business, but it didn't seem to do that. Whatever magic he worked must have been strong because I never heard anything bad about him, even from the family or friends of a girl he had romanced and left behind.

Just after he settled in at Sunset he said he'd need an assistant manager because of the long work hours. He had a woman picked out, someone whom I did not know but who seemed the right type when I met her. I did wonder if she and Errol were lovers and it turned out to be so.

Eileen stayed for a year (a long time for Errol) then there was Lisa and now there's Sharon. They've all been competent and nice and, though the arrangement is irregular and wouldn't appear I am sure in any manual on 'best business practice', it seems to have worked. I suppose there are some people in town who disapprove but I take the view that it's harming no-one. There are far worse things happening around us I'm sure – and meanwhile business at Sunset is booming.

***

I like going to the motel; I go about nine in the morning. This is the busiest time of the day, with people checking out and staff beginning to clean the rooms – the worst time to try to talk with a manager you would think, especially a hands-on type like Errol Makim – and we do get a lot of interruptions.

I used to phone before coming to the motel but Errol kept telling me to come unannounced. Then I turned up at quiet times, like after lunch, but he didn't like that either; he told me – I remember his saying it – that if *he* owned a motel he'd want to see it when it was at its busiest. So I took his suggestion and I am glad I did; I get more idea of how things are going from fifteen hectic minutes than I would from an hour of quiet talk. I even get dragged into taking phone bookings and advising people on their trips, and enjoy it.

***

It's interesting that although Errol's been managing the motel for three years he isn't looking for a break. He has holidays of course but what I mean is that he wants to *continue with the job*. I've talked with other motel owners and they say it's very hard to find someone who will stay year after year – and if they do stay on they tend to become irritable.

44

I've met managers like that when I've stayed somewhere. I used to think they were in the wrong job – and I do think it's a job that suits only some people. It wouldn't suit me; I am a people person to some extent I suppose but I like my solitude too and you don't seem to get enough of that when you run a motel. Anyway now, when I meet an owner or manager who is a bit 'short', I think he probably just needs a break. Not like Errol.

***

I do not know how good a 'boss' I am but I have had a lot of experience in business and have employed a lot of people. I tell new employees that it is not *I* who pays their wages but our customers. The good ones grasp this concept; I think Errol *was born knowing it*. I am so lucky he walked through my door five years ago.

***

Last week I was in Manningham when Errol rang me at my hotel. He was down in the city for the day too and would I meet him in the lounge for lunch and a drink? He wanted to introduce me to someone.

So I met his ex-wife – and we had a really nice time. She enjoyed the stories Errol and I told about life out west. When she left I got a hug but Errol got a bigger hug and a kiss. Seems we all like Errol.

SEVEN

A GOOD DAY'S WORK

I am not driving particularly fast this morning but I keep hitting birds. I try slowing down but this has no effect – even when I drop right back to forty. Blowing the horn doesn't work either – the birds seem determined to ignore me. Three times I have gone right through flocks of galahs that have stayed on the road until it was too late.

I've noticed this phenomenon on other occasions but mostly just before sunset. I remember one afternoon I hit virtually every crested pigeon that was on the road. I didn't want to of course – hated it – but those birds, that are usually so adept at avoiding cars, had sat that day as if mesmerised. It was at sorghum harvest time and I put it down to the fact that they had been gorging on the grain that had spilled from trucks, and perhaps they had been just too heavy to make a quick getaway. Except that didn't explain why they had *delayed* their attempts to escape; it was almost as if they were drugged. *Could* they have been, I have wondered, by something in the grain?

I see quite a few magpies this morning, but they are different. Of all the birds I think the black and white ones look after themselves best. You never hit a magpie.

My daughter-in-law Sally had phoned the previous night to say that buyers were due to call at our property today to look at cattle but that Ralph had hurt his back and wouldn't be able to do the muster. They would have to cancel their visit unless I could come out from town.

"It's just a pulled muscle Dad. They were moving one of those heavy pipes in the yards and he tripped over a fig root and instead of just letting his end go he tried to hold it up. Stupid man. He just needs to rest it for a couple of days but he's too sore now. He can't even turn over without whimpering." She had chuckled; Ralph, my energetic, quicksilver second son, wouldn't be a patient patient.

***

I reach the property by eight-thirty but the buyers are not due till eleven, so I can spend some time with Ralph and Sally and the kids. Ralph is now walking, but very stiffly, and he grimaces when he turns. Sally makes us a coffee; by contrast she is brisk and cheerful.

"We told them they were a very even lot and they said in that case we wouldn't need to put them in the yards. Holding them in a corner of a paddock would do. They're in 'Little Creek'." Ralph catches my eye and we both grin. "What?"

"It's their first ploy Sally," I tell her. "If I don't like their offer – and I'm sure I won't – they will then tell me there is actually quite a lot of variation in the cattle and we'll have to take them to the yards and draft them up."

"And that even if they do come up a bit on the best ones they'll have to come back on the others," Ralph adds, "and the price will probably work out the same, overall."

"Yep. By the way, do we know these hombres?"

"No – first time here."

"Good. Do we have any weights?"

"I weighed a bunch of them last week." Ralph hands me a list of figures.

"Wise move."

"And I put the scales out of sight in the shed."

"Even wiser. Who taught you these tricks?"

***

Sally lends me her own horse Rocky and by a quarter to eleven I have the mob nicely settled in a corner of 'Little Creek', with the help of Craig the young ringer. I am ready in more ways than one; I know the current auction rates, and Ralph, Sally and I have agreed on our prices. I also know we still have plenty of sorghum crop left, so we can hold the cattle over.

The men arrive, we introduce ourselves, and even as we shake hands they are casting their eyes over the cattle. We have bought the best Santa Gertrudis and Droughtmaster bulls we could afford over the last twenty years, and these steers show the benefit. John and Brendan give no sign of it but I am confident they are impressed; I doubt if they will have seen a better mob of well finished, well bred cattle. They display the usual mien of professional cattle buyers however, friendly but non-committal, in no way seeming keen to buy.

***

Their first offer comes and I frown. "I'm sure they're worth more than that. We've been looking at the auctions in Manningham. They seem to be very strong." Then I add, as if the thought has just struck me, "they're near your works. If we trucked them in you could bid on them there."

This idea has absolutely no appeal. Once word got around that three hundred heavy prime were coming in from the Run every big meat buyer in central Queensland would be interested. There would be no chance of these men setting their own prices then.

There is actually, they inform me now, some variation amongst them. "We probably should take them to the yards and draft them up. We might be able to come up a bit on the best of them but we'd have to come back on some of the others," John says, very regretfully.

"Yes," says Brendan, "and actually it'll probably average out at much the same," he says to me, and to John he adds, as if in afterthought, "we've got to be at the Flemings by two, haven't we?"

"We'd better get a move on then" I say, and urge Rocky forward; I have heard it all before. Craig and I push the cattle along the fence towards the yards. Within half an hour we have them in and our visitors are working the drafting gates. I borrow their Nissan and go back to the house for a thermos of tea.

"How's it going?" Sally asks.

"Oh, the usual. They're drafting them now. They're six cents a kilogram under but I think they'll come up." Six cents would mean more than thirty dollars a head.

"Or we won't sell?"

"Or we won't sell. Next time it's your turn to do this."

"Oh no, I couldn't do it. It's a man's game. It seems silly to me, you all *know* the values and you all know what the results will be."

"Ah, but sometimes these guys realise we *don't* know the values. And sometimes, even when we do, we give in."

"*You* don't. I should go down and warn those men."

"Too late. We're best friends already. But I might take a few sandwiches with me. This could take a while."

When I arrive back John is on his satellite phone, and I assume he is reporting on the situation to his boss. The drafting has been completed and of course the men have done a good job. Each of the three groups is certainly more even now – but this has really been only an exercise; at the regular fat sale in Manningham these steers, in my opinion, would sell pen after pen – undrafted – at the one price per kilogram, and for more than the figure the men first offered. In fact, a line as big and as good as ours generally creates a buzz that can push prices up as an auction proceeds.

"You've done a nice job" I say. Sixty percent of the cattle have made it into their 'top' line. "But you can't expect to have the tops for that sort of money." I ask for ten cents above their first offer for these and, a little to my surprise, they agree quite quickly. They have decided on this while I was away.

"We'll take these too," John says, indicating the next largest group, "but they're a bit light. We don't like handling anything under five hundred kilograms."

They don't believe we have scales – good on you Ralph. "They'd be *over* five" I say.

"No way," and they look at each other and shake their heads – sadly – as if this were a matter of personal sorrow to them. They're good.

"Why don't we weigh some Mr. Watson?" innocent young Craig suggests.

"Good idea."

The men do not show any reaction to the news that we have scales, and in fact help us lift them out of the shed and place them on the floor of the crush. The first beast of this line registers five hundred and sixty kilograms and the next half dozen average five hundred and forty. The men call a halt at that. They still want to drop five cents off the top price but I dig in at two and, again quite quickly, they agree. I am on a roll.

"We definitely can't take these though," they tell me, indicating the third group. "They're not finished. We'd have to feed them for at least six weeks."

I doubt this; take out the tops from the whole mob and the remainder would still sell at Manningham as prime. I count them and there are fifty-six, *exactly* the number that would fill a double decker. They do want them – but they want a bargain.

"We have plenty of sorghum left. We can put them back," I say, and move as if to let them out into the holding yard.

"We *could* take them, but we'd have to come back a fair bit." We begin the real haggle now; they offer ten cents less than the previous price – I say two – they move to eight. I concede to three – and there we stop.

***

We pour cups of tea and open up the sandwiches and talk of other things: the State of Origin, the Dry. Brendan tells me he used to ride with my eldest son Bill at Pony Club.

***

When we get back to business we settle on a five cent drop. They use their phone to book trucks for the next day, ask to be told when we have another mob for sale, and are on their way by one-thirty.

***

In the evening, I sit in the homestead's big kitchen while Sally cooks and Ralph, a bit more comfortable, lets the boys climb all over him on the old lounge that we have brought in for him from another room. It's a scene that this father and grandfather relishes.

"We'll feed these two and get them off to bed before we eat," Sally says.

"That Rocky of yours is terrific," I tell her. "You've done a good job on him." Sally is a good horsewoman.

"It's mostly him. He's a natural."

Ralph has been playing with a small calculator. "You did well Dad. You got an extra sixteen thousand dollars out of those robbers. Not a bad day's work."

***

Early the next morning I hear on the ABC that Japan has announced two large new beef tenders. Prices are expected to jump immediately – and John and Brendan would have known this.

I help Craig and the truckies load the cattle, have an early lunch and begin the drive back to town. I listen to the Country Hour and learn that during the morning's sale at Manningham prices have increased *twenty cents*.

***

I come round a bend and see two magpies standing in the road. They see me but I know I do not need to slow down; you never hit a magpie.

EIGHT

MAGGIE

I like bantams, especially bantam hens. There is something about the look of them that is very appealing to me – the curves of neck and tail, the many colours of them, and the way their feathers so perfectly overlay each other – and those bright eyes, and that quick appreciation of any situation – their busy ways. They are efficient little managers of their lives, and of course brilliant rearers of chicks.

I keep quite a number of real laying hens, Rhode Island Reds and the big black Australorps, but I always have a few bantams as well, to hatch settings of eggs and – well frankly – just because I like them so much. They are much friendlier than my other hens; if any chooks gather around me when I am sitting on my back steps it is invariably these little ladies. I put grain on my boots and they peck it off; some even jump onto my knee and take it from my hand, even allowing me to stroke them.

One tiny orange ball of fluff has a brood of six chicks at present; strictly speaking they are an Australorp's, but though they are quite the wrong colour, and already half the size of their foster mother – at just two weeks – this little one believes they are all her own work, and is fiercely protective of them.

This hen was the favourite of my friend Maggie. When she called in on one of her walks around town, she would sit with me on these steps, or on the bench under the Peppercorn, and Orange would always jump up on her lap, and stay there as long as the visit lasted.

Maggie asked me not long ago if the hen had ever reared chicks and when I said no she begged me to allow it. "Just because she's little doesn't mean she couldn't be a good mother." When the hen went broody just a few weeks ago I did give her a setting; she hatched them all, and *is* rearing them very well – but sadly my friend will never see them.

***

I remember first sighting Maggie Fitch in the main street of our town shortly after I moved into the district in the early 1970's; she was the smallest woman I had ever seen, just 130 centimetres – perhaps even less. She was wearing jodhpurs and a long sleeved shirt, which I would learn was her favourite attire. Her hair, black and very long, hung down her back in one thick plait.

Locals told me she rode racehorses for her father, exercising and helping to train them. She also did casual work for people, secretarial and gardening. She never drove, but walked everywhere, and briskly. She had a somewhat severe expression but it broke into a nice smile when she said hello. Bright eyes. She would I suppose have then been about thirty.

While I was living for the next twenty years or so out on our cattle property I would see her only occasionally, at a race meeting or when I came to town, but when I settled here after my wife died I saw her quite often: still moving quickly – a little dynamo.

She had kept her hair long, but now wore it up, coiled on top of her head and held in place with one of those large Spanish combs. She also now wore skirts, unusual ones that probably were specially made; they were tight at the waist, long, and very full at the hem. They were often of a heavy material, and when she walked, with her long brisk stride, they swung. She wore Cubans, those elastic sided riding boots that have a high heel; she still wore long-sleeved shirts, not blouses. The effect was Argentinian – imagine a small female gaucho.

***

Perhaps a year after I had relocated myself here, and with my growing business interests taking a lot of my time, I advertised in our local paper for someone to clean my house and do the washing and ironing, and the first person to answer the ad was Maggie.

I was surprised. For one thing there was her age; I had envisaged a younger woman, a stay-at-home mother perhaps; Maggie then would have been in her fifties. Also, I thought the modest amount I was offering would not have been attractive to her – it was generally known that she had been left comfortably off by her family – but when I raised the subject of pay, a little embarrassedly, she brushed it aside. "Doesn't matter. You need help and I've got the time."

The big question in my mind though concerned her stature; would she actually be able to handle the work? Could she reach the clothes that were at the bottom of my washing machine, or stand up above my ironing board? As for washing the taller windows…….

***

She came once or sometimes twice a week, worked the whole morning – and managed everything perfectly. She found herself a sturdy wooden box to stand on in the laundry and at the ironing board, and she used my folding steps for dusting high shelves and mantelpieces. The top sections of my sash windows *were* beyond her but I had forbidden that anyhow because I was worried she might fall; we did those windows as a team.

***

Employer and employee quickly became friends, and she shared her history with me. Her parents had not married until they were in their late thirties, by which time Reg, who had been a stockman then overseer on one of our bigger district cattle properties, had drawn a block in a land ballot just to the east of the town. He worked hard on the place, Maggie told me, but had just got it into reasonable order when a worsening hip problem made it difficult for him to continue, and they decided to sell.

Though the property was small by district standards it fetched a high price, largely because of its proximity to town (but I know it well, and it is also very good country.) The trio was able to live off interest on the invested proceeds, in a house here in town.

Reg Fitch was a keen horseman, and had trained a few racehorses for local people as a hobby, and after he moved to town he decided to do more of this. He employed a succession of strappers and jockeys, with Maggie also riding and exercising the horses.

"I remember Maggie at those race meetings," Mary Carmody told me. "She handled those horses like they were farmyard pets. She didn't ride them in the actual races though; I don't think female jockeys were allowed then."

"Was she always small? At school?"

"No, not as a young girl – primary school. Average I would have said. Oh, a little below; Reg and Mildred were both short. No – it seemed to be from about twelve or so she just stopped growing. She filled out in the other ways, but she stayed tiny .What is she – four feet?"

"I'd say. And never married?"

"No. No boyfriend either, that I can remember. I suppose, being so tiny; pity though, she would have made someone a very good wife."

Once when Maggie told me that someone we both knew was a good mother and I said that *she* would have made a good one, she joked that she wouldn't have had room to carry a baby for nine months.

"Do you know why you didn't grow any taller?"

"No. And none of the doctors did either. A mystery." She said it in a matter of fact tone – in no way sad or bitter – but I suppose there must have been times………

***

I learned a lot about the history of our town from Maggie, as she passed on stories she had heard from the old timers. We'd talk about world affairs too; she was well informed, and certainly had opinions. They were delivered with firmness – perhaps a little dogmatically – but she did listen to my attempts to put alternative ones. I gained the impression that she did not often exchange serious views or even have good talks with many other people.

***

She stopped working for me about five years ago, when she was approaching seventy. I had been trying to persuade her to stop for years before but I think she may just have enjoyed the contact. She still dropped in once a week though.

And now, unexpectedly, my friend is no more. Taking to her bed with a bad cold, she had contracted pneumonia. She lived alone, and none of us had thought to check on her until it was too late. I share the blame for that.

***

I have one more thing I need to do for her now; I am her executor. Her wishes were simple; as she had no living relatives I was to sell her house and give the proceeds and the rest of her funds to the local schools. I could dispose of her personal effects as I saw fit.

I decided to ask our mutual friend Mary to come with me to Maggie's house while I catalogued her possessions. I thought that if there were saleable items there she might have a better idea of their values and how we might realise on them. Also, frankly, I was uncomfortable at the thought of going through Maggie's home and possessions on my own; I wanted another person with me, preferably a woman, and Mary was ideal.

We soon saw that the crockery and cutlery was just of an every-day quality and in addition there seemed to be no special collectables or display items. The furniture was 1920's and fairly plain; I thought that we might as well give everything to our local 'Vinnies'.

***

Mary began going through the clothing in the wardrobe of what was obviously Maggie's bedroom. She said that everything was so tiny they would not fit anybody else. I went out into the kitchen to start boxing up some of the crockery.

A few minutes later she called to me, some excitement in her voice; I found her in the second bedroom. She was standing before the open doors of a built-in wardrobe that extended right along one wall, and was holding a garment across each arm.

"These are gorgeous Hugh. Look at the beading on this." She held up a long black dress that glittered even under the dim light of the small overhead bulb. "And the embroidery on this!"

She laid the garments on the bed and brought out two more. "Oh, beautiful."

"I can smell camphor."

"Yes, she looked after them. I can't see any moth damage, or even any wear. They're immaculate. And they are full size. Maggie never wore any of these."

"They look pretty old."

"1950's and 60's. Oh, you don't get work like this now." She held up another dress to the light. "Hugh, they're beautifully made."

"This is a mystery then. Who did they belong to?"

Mary stood still for a moment, then turned to me. "I don't know, but I think her mother could have made these. She was a dressmaker and had a very good reputation. My own mother had things made by her. But dressmakers don't usually do beading and embroidery."

"Could Maggie have done that?"

"Yes. She was very good at craftwork. Very clever with those little hands."

"But if they were made for clients – how would Maggie end up with them?"

"Well – I don't know – perhaps she just asked people if she could have them after they had worn them a few times …."

"But they are immaculate you said. Hardly worn at all."

"Hugh, the women who had these made for them would have had money. Like my mother. Like me. We don't wear good outfits over and over, or even special ones. *Particularly* special ones. No, she wouldn't have had any problem getting these back."

"So – why?"

"I suppose we will never know for sure."

"Well – in memory of her mother? Keepsakes. And she *had* done some of the work..."

"Or – Hugh – dreaming of what might have been? If she had grown to normal height, been a 'normal' person, she would have worn things like these." She took another garment from the rack. "This is a ball gown. Shantung." She held it up against herself. "You could wear this today. But little Maggie didn't go to balls. She never did. She must have thought no-one would dance with her. Sad...."

We were silent a moment then I shook myself up. "If these are so good maybe we can sell them?"

Mary turned towards me. "Do you have complete say about what to do with them?"

"Yes. Why?"

"I think we should keep them."

"*Keep* them?"

"In our museum. A new section – 'Social History'. That place is too masculine anyhow. All those implements and tools!"

"Well – I am on the Museum Committee. We *could*....." I looked up at the ceiling. "Would that be okay Maggie?"

"Of course it would. And if that penny-pinching committee of your's won't buy some decent cabinets I will pay for them myself. These have to be properly displayed. And *I'll* have the information cards made. I know someone who's fantastic on old fashions. And I think it actually won't be too hard to find out who used to own these.

This will be very interesting."

Mary went on pulling dresses out; I was leaning against a tall chest and for something to do I pulled open the top drawer. In it were two packages side by side, wrapped in tissue paper. I took out one, laid it on the bed and unwrapped what looked to be a shirt – very small – yellow, with a diagonal brown stripe.

"Oh," Mary said, "a jockey's silk."

"It's tiny."

"It was hers, look" and she pointed to 'Maggie' embroidered on the left shoulder. I took the second package out and unwrapped it.

"Another one. Identical."

"Not quite" Mary said. She pointed to the name 'Tom.'

"Who would that have been?"

"Tom – Tom – " Mary repeated to herself. "There *was* a Tom. One of the young jockeys Reg employed. Tom – oh, what was his name? I remember he came from the coast. He eventually went back to the family farm there – a dairy. Yes, he used to ride at the meetings. He was good looking too, a nice open face. He was very popular. And Maggie would have spent a lot of time with him."

She picked up one of the silks and took it to the light. "They're nicely done. Her mother would have made these too. And Maggie might have done the names." She turned towards me. "Hugh, do you think they….?" She raised her eyebrows.

"What?" but I knew; I'd seen Mary before when she thought she had discovered a love secret of one of her friends.

"Well – side by side in the drawer – that's a clue. And why not? They were together a lot – they were young......."

"She never mentioned him to me."

"Why would she – so long ago….?"

"Well, we did talk about life. And love. A bit."

"Oh Hugh, let's keep these too." She placed the silk on the bed beside the other and moved the sleeves so that that they were touching. She smiled. "Holding hands."

***

When I saw Mary a few days later she told me she had taken all the clothes to her own dressmaker – "just to fix any little thing" – and that she had already tracked down the owners of some of the dresses. I promised to talk to the Museum Committee.

"We'll need a lot of display cases." she warned. "And I'm going to need a special little one for the two silks."

***

Now as I sit under my Jacaranda I am thinking about my little departed friend. Orange is beside me with her chicks – the chicks that she thinks are entirely hers. I have decided to rename her Maggie – and acquire a bantam rooster, and call him Tom.

NINE

MOTHER AND SON

When I look back over what I have written so far, I would have to admit that there is very little in the way of *story line*; I have just been 'colouring in' this picture of my town, and introducing you to my friends. And I fear things will not get much better – you have yet to meet Georgia and Kitty and Isobel.

I also acknowledge that the *pace* is anything but breathtaking – but then I am of an age where my days are, to say the least, not crowded with incident and adventure. They are still full of interest to *me* though, and it is my hope – my fervent hope – that I have been making them of interest to others.

One of my odder pursuits is an interest in classical Indian music, especially long pieces; some of the ragas in my collection are an hour long (and I know that in India some recitals last *all day.*) I was once advised that, to aid in surrendering to those strange melodies and subtle rhythms, I should imagine I was floating on a long and majestic river, as it moved towards its destination on some distant shore; it was useful advice, and I still follow it.

I hope readers will stay on the meandering river that is 'Redspear'; it is certainly far from majestic, and might even occasionally come to a halt, but I feel sure it – and we – will reach a shoreline.

**

A Sunday morning now and Mary, her manager Robbie Riley, Helen and I are in Mary's apartment, sharing a quite sumptuous morning tea. It is a celebration.

Mary, Robbie and I are the Redspear team in a state-wide general knowledge quiz competition. We competed the night before here in town and comfortably beat off three other district teams. Helen Carruthers stood in for Robbie on this occasion because of his laryngitis; he listened to the radio broadcast of it.

"I suppose you knew it was Kanchenjunga?" Mary accuses Robbie, and I think of course he did; he probably knows the exact height of every bloody mountain in the world. He'd have got the tricky one about the Constitution too; if he hadn't had to drop out we would have got close to a perfect score.

His legs do a kind of shuffle and he smirks, and if you did not know him you'd feel like tipping your cup of tea over him – but you have to move your legs like that when they're long and confined to a wheelchair, and a smirk is really only what an ordinary smile looks like when it is coming from a face that life has done its best to rearrange. More about that a little later.

Our "Gazette" will carry a report about our win in two day's time. I know what it will say because I have just written it.

VICTORY FOR REDSPEAR

On Saturday our team in the State "Know All" competition came out convincing winners of the Mid-Western division before a capacity crowd of three hundred people in the Old Shire Hall. Mary Carmody, Helen

66

Carruthers and Hugh Watson managed fifty-six points out of a possible sixty to end the evening twenty-four points ahead of our nearest rival Gemfields. The other teams were Coalfields and Three Rivers. (There is no truth in the rumour that the editor has been bribed by them not to reveal their scores!)

The win sets our team up for the Central finals in Manningham in a few weeks' time. Readers will recall that last year Redspear won the Central Finals and went to the State Finals which we also won in a dead heat with Darling Downs. On that occasion, through sponsorship, a total of $130,000 was returned to charities in our district.

Helen Carruthers easily held her place in the team on Saturday even though she was a late substitution for regular member Robbie Riley, who had contracted laryngitis during the week. Helen said afterwards she had enjoyed the night. "I am just glad I didn't let the team down. I was lucky some of my questions were on subjects I knew something about, but Robbie can run rings around me."

Robbie Riley will be part of the team once again at the Central Final in Manningham.

I had written the piece the way I did, emphasising Robbie's undeniable place in our team, as much for *him* as our readership. Patronising of me I suppose, to think I needed to do that; if ever a 'disabled' person does not require his confidence being boosted it is Robbie.

***

Jenny Porter came to our town as a single schoolteacher. I remember her as quite engaging in a one to one conversation but not *outgoing* – certainly not an extrovert – so it surprised many of us when she became engaged to Boy Riley, a mechanic, who you would say was the opposite type – your typical story-telling, gregarious young Irishman, all shining black hair, smiling eyes and a ready laugh.

Within a year of marriage Robbie had come along but then, within a few months of that, tragedy. While Boy was doing some work on a bulldozer on a property, a prop gave way and he was crushed to death.

Jenny got all the support we could give her but it was just the beginning of trouble for that little family. Robbie contracted a polio-like virus when he was three that left his legs virtually paralysed. Eventually he was able to walk but only with a pair of sticks; they proved too slow for the boy, and from when he was just a year or so older he went everywhere in a wheelchair.

***

One morning, as Jenny was backing her car out of the driveway and Robbie, then about eight years old, was racing her to the gate – a game he often played – he lost control of the chair and pitched sideways into her path. The car's rear wheel passed over his head, fracturing many bones. Surgeons did a wonderful job on his face but he was left with disfigurement – a tilt to one side, and eyes somehow of different sizes.

The boy became very self-conscious and refused to go back to school, and Jenny left the Education Department to do private tutoring, so she could teach him at home. Over the following years he passed all his exams, and, Jenny told me, without doing any study at all. He was very bright; she said that by the age of ten he could pick up any book on any subject and understand it (an attribute that has served him and us very well now in the quiz.)

Robbie quit school as soon as it was legal – I think that was fourteen – and more or less did nothing for two years. At a school meeting one night, a worried Jenny asked me if I could help. It was not long after I had bought the Gazette and I wondered if we might be able to find a useful place there for Robbie. We badly needed someone to proof read, and Robbie proved to be brilliant at it – fast and accurate. "He's terrific," Kent said, "and he can write too. Why don't we get him to do some reports?" Robbie was soon a regular sight flying around town in his wheelchair, with pen and pad and little tape recorder.

We put him on full-time and whenever I called in at the Gazette I could see what an asset he was; he could interview, write, sub-edit, and do layouts – everything. He had such a good mind that he seemed to learn all the facets of running a paper in no time at all.

The fact that he used a wheelchair inside the building was no obstacle to him. Kent and I modified a few doors and passageways to help him but that was all; when he was asked to man the front desk he would prop himself up there on his sticks. He was very good with the public too, quick and helpful.

***

I learned from Jenny that he had begun studying at home for the Higher School Certificate. "It's a miracle Hugh. He is *so* motivated. I'm helping him but he's exhausting." He could not have had better assistance though, and he finished with a score that would have qualified him for any course at any university.

During the year he had developed an interest in finance and he now began a distance uni course in commerce. He still did general reporting work for the paper, but now he began to do features on business matters. He started a series of articles on successful local businessmen, both farmers and townspeople. He began to study the share market too, and started a regular column on dealing; people began to approach him for advice, offering to pay for it. He asked me how his employer felt about that and I not only approved but became a client.

He seemed to have a very good grasp of what business was about. Even some of the people from his interview series gave him retainers to advise *them*. His income grew; I think that within a year he was probably earning more from these sources than from us, and over the following two years, while still doing his degree – in which he was getting Distinctions – his total income probably trebled.

***

One day Mary Carmody rang; "I want to talk to you". She always speaks like that – it sounds like a command, though she would be surprised if she heard me say that – but I always do 'obey', because it is invariably interesting, and sometimes profitable.

Mary had always managed her own business dealings, down to the tiniest detail, but she was by now in her late seventies and possibly wearying of the constant attention her multitude of ventures demanded. Now – did I know of someone who could work for her, and was Robbie really as good as people were saying? Straight to the point.

The long and short of it is that Robbie, still just twenty-one, was made the offer one cannot refuse – a generous wage, and incentives for results – and Mary gained someone who, in just a few years, has transformed her considerable fortune into a monumental one. In the process, Robbie, still only twenty-eight, has also done very well for himself.

***

Robbie seems to expect the rest of us to make no allowances for his disability and appearance, and we do try. Most of the time it is easy because he is such an energetic, capable person. I realise though that I still have something of a protective attitude towards him – the father in me perhaps – and this rises up again when Mary rings me the following day to say that a television producer based at the coast had been in the quiz audience and wants now to cover the next round at Manningham, with the proviso that the team stay the same.

"No!"

She sighs. "That's what I said. I explained about Robbie being sick but he spouted some claptrap about wanting to 'promote a higher profile for rural women'."

"And Robbie has an odd face and Helen is a knockout."

"She does come up very well on television. I saw her when they covered the race meeting last year."

I pause; I am thinking about the woman on the phone. If anyone has an odd face, and well and truly knows it, it is Mary. The fire in the hotel when she was a young woman all but burned away the features on one side. Her friends are accustomed to the disfigurement but I could imagine a television producer being concerned. And then, if he had to think of adding Robbie.....

"Where are you on this?"

"With you. It's Robbie, you and me. But Hugh – Robbie has *agreed*."

"You've already *asked* him?"

"Don't get angry. No, he *offered* to stand down."

Mary says that after Grainger had been to see her that morning she had gone to Robbie's office. She says she had just told him about the producer and his interest in televising the next round and was getting round to telling him about his request – and that she had said no – when Robbie jumped ahead of her and said that he supposed that the producer wanted Helen to stay in the team and if he did, it was perfectly fine by him.

"I hope you argued against it?"

"I did. I said I would rather no TV than do that. I offered to drop out myself. I meant it. But Hugh – he really doesn't seem to care. Will you go and see him?"

***

Robbie is leaning back in his sprung chair when I go into his office, his big arms behind his neck. Before I say anything he says, smiling, "it's alright Hugh. Really. I'm fine with it."

"But Robbie..."

"They want her on. And she'll look great."

He closes his eyes and leans back. He is smiling; it certainly does seem as if he does not care.

"I have, if you like, a face saver," and grimaces at his own joke. "Why not remind them that our chief aim is to raise funds for charity and say that you're worried we might not do as well with Helen."

I think about it. "They might come in as sponsors."

He nods. "Could be worth ten thousand."

"More, if we win."

"Yes. Easily. And Helen *is* good anyhow."

I laugh. "No wonder Mary does so well."

***

I had given in, but someone else had not.

Sitting opposite me in my lounge room Robbie's mother Jenny gives me a long and vigorous dressing down; I do not know why I ever believed her to be mild mannered. In a Force 10 battering Jenny calls Mary Carmody, Helen Carruthers and me cowards and moral bankrupts. I do not dare to interrupt; this is a lioness defending her cub.

When she seems to have finished, I ask nervously if I may phone Mary, and when that even more formidable woman says she is busy I surprise all of us by ordering her attendance.

Jenny is more restrained in her language with Mary present but the gist of her message is the same. I attempt a defence.

"Jenny, we did tell the television people that we three were the team."

"But they ignored you. They wanted Helen and you went along with it."

"No, we disagreed."

"It needs saying," says Mary. "I think they felt television could handle one 'face' but not two."

"But you..." Jenny stops herself.

"Yes I know, and I offered to withdraw. Robbie might slightly alarm the horses but I can stampede them."

It's a gracious contribution; Jenny touches Mary's hand.

"They really want Helen, Jenny. She *was* very good," I say.

"I know, but they had no right to ask this!"

"I agree and Mary and Helen and I all said no. But Jenny, it was Robbie who said yes. Insisted."

We are all silent. I am realising we should have stood firm; I should not even have listened to Robbie's plan to get more sponsorship – but the television company had agreed so quickly to his proposal for sponsorship that events seemed to pass out of our control. The silence stretches.

"The worst of it is that we can't change it now," Mary says at last.

"Why not? Why can't you just tell them what you want?"

"Because – we had to sign a contract."

"A contract!?"

"An agreement. Television does this apparently. The high-ups or the lawyers insist on it."

"To do what?"

"To appear in the next one at Manningham and if we win that, in the capital. Hugh, Helen and I. There's money involved. Some extra sponsorship. We'd be liable if we broke it."

At this Jenny is beginning to look combative again. I can see how this might look to her; her son has been bought out.

"Jenny, it was Rob who recommended signing the contract." I say. "He was very positive. Believe me please."

Jenny looks at the floor for a long while then looks up and nods, but there are tears there. I offer drinks but she says no, she has a private teaching appointment.

***

Now it is five-thirty and getting dark. I have put on one of the garden lights and am sitting on the verandah in one of my canvas squatter's chairs. My two fierce guard dogs lie at my feet while next door's half grown kitten plays with their tails.

The confrontation with Jenny has shaken me. I feel I have let her and Robbie down, and perhaps let myself down too. My ritual late afternoon whisky is more than usually welcome.

A car goes past, slowly. Smoke rises from chimneys into a cloudless sky and I know we will have quite a cold night. I imagine Jenny herself might also be sitting like this on her own verandah, and I wonder how *she* is feeling.

I tell myself I have not lost her friendship and I certainly hope not. I would feel diminished; it has been an honour to know that woman.

TEN

BOBBO

"Hugh, you know my crow?" Mary, accosting me in the main street.

"Yes – we've met."

"Well the damn thing is following me!"

"Where?"

"On walks. Around the town. You know how I like to have a stroll on a Sunday afternoon. Well yesterday I went with Elsie Chatham and he came too. He flew from one telegraph pole to the next the whole way. For an hour and a half! Sybil Fox asked us in for a cool drink and when we came out he was still there!"

"You're sure it was..."

"Of course I am. Do you think I don't know my own crow? When I got back to the hotel he flew straight up to the gazebo and demanded that meat I give him."

"Do you mind?"

"Well I do. It's....." She paused. "It's like being stalked."

"Mary, it's a *crow*."

"I know," she laughed. "But when I started feeding him I didn't count on this."

***

That was my way of introducing you to yet another of my friends – and someone whom birds and animals *do* regularly follow; he *talks* to them and for all I know *they talk to him*. Bobbo certainly acts as if they do – and my own animals definitely behave quite differently when he is around; it's as if there is some extra level of communication happening there.

***

He was christened Robert I suppose, but for as long as I have known him, and that has been since he was a baby, he has been Bobbo. His father Clive used to work for us out on the 'Run'; Bobbo came into the world in the same week as our youngest, Nicholas.

Bobbo was too young to be a playmate of our other three children, but he and Nick were inseparable when they were very little. Bobbo lives with his parents here in town now, and Nick as you know in Brisbane, but they are still close. Whenever Nick comes back to town they get together.

They are both twenty-four but Bobbo is still a boy and always will be. He is what people used to call "slow" – I would say he has a mental age of just eight or nine – his comprehension is at that level. But he has a knowledge of some things – natural things mostly – that astonishes me sometimes.

He has a sweet nature, and I love him as I do my own four; if ever Clive and Rita find they can no longer care for him, I will do so.

***

I nod off to sleep in bed at night very easily but also very often wake early – sometimes as early as three or so. I get up then and

76

do some bookwork, and at such times while I am at my desk I will sometimes hear a light tap on the window. I let Bobbo in and he helps himself to some milk from the fridge, and some biscuits or cake.

He knows how to put on my music CD's and he nearly always selects one of my Indian ones; Bobbo has a passion for them. He will sit motionless through the longest piece.

I do not allow my dogs inside at night – actually I try not to have them inside at any time – but when Bobbo is here on these occasions they will not be denied. They seem to dig my Indian music too – at least when they can listen to it with their friend.

***

When I am driving about the town at night I often see the boy walking the streets, or standing and watching the occupants of houses through uncurtained windows. People only know he's there if they happen to go outside for some reason. They are never alerted by a barking dog; dogs do not bark at Bobbo.

No-one seems to get upset about his nocturnal rambles but then we all know him. He even hitches a ride at night in the police patrol car. "I like Constable Shane and Constable Damian," he has told me. "They buy me ice-creams. I don't like the sergeant but."

Sergeant Hagan is, in fact, the only person in town who makes a fuss over Bobbo. He rang me once to ask me to try to get him to stop the night walks. I did nothing; I did not like Hagan's tone. A hard man – and an unhappy one I think.

***

I have tried to persuade people to give Bobbo some paid work. He is fine, I have told them, if they just work out first what jobs he can do; at my place he looks after my dogs and chooks when I am away, and mows the lawns. I do have to go through the mower starting routine with him each time; I have learned not to write things like that down but to do a series of illustrations. My drawing skills have improved a lot since Bobbo began doing jobs for me.

At my urging, Helen at "The Bauhinias" and my manager Errol at "The Sunset" have found work for him in their gardens. The only concern they have had is over the lad's too frank interest in some of the guests. Not surprisingly, some people become a bit agitated at being scrutinised at close quarters by a large silent young man. Errol and Helen now ask him to come during the middle hours of the day, when there are fewer guests around.

Helen has told me her golden retriever Prince ignores her completely when Bobbo is there – as my two cattle dogs do when Bobbo is here. They sit with their heads in his lap as he fondles their ears. Any words he says seem to fall on them like some drugging rain.

Old Mary had more difficulty finding work for him at her big hotel – there is not all that much for him to do outside. "Do you know what I do Hugh? I get him to clean and polish the silver. And the chandelier. I was a bit wary of that because, well, you know how big it is – and how hard it would be to replace those drops – but he is *so* careful."

***

Bobbo does something else I did not learn about until recently; he helps at the railway station yards, unloading and loading cattle, and feeding hay to any that have to be held there for any time. I asked him once to tell me what he does there but he told me instead about a bird. As best as I can remember, this is what he said. (I will try to capture his way of talking; there are usually many pauses.)

"My crow always comes to me – he doesn't go to the men – sometimes they say 'there's your crow Bobbo' but it isn't him – isn't that funny they don't know. He likes corned meat. One man Phil says I should catch him and put him in a cage but that's bad – how could he fly? Birds are lucky, they can go anywhere.....″

My belief in the magical powers of Bobbo are such that I wouldn't be surprised if *he* could fly. Would it be up high, perhaps with the brolgas that sometimes circle above Redspear? Or would he be nocturnal – swooping silently with the owls?

I asked him once why he liked to go out at night but he said simply "I'm awake." He added that he *sees more* at night and I wondered what exactly he meant by that. Was he referring to the lighted interiors of houses – or the night birds and animals?

He must know that he is 'different'; perhaps at night – in the dark – he feels safer.

***

His hearing is phenomenal. He will tell me he can hear my phone ringing even when we are standing right down at my back gate, some fifty metres from the house. I have good hearing but I can only just hear the thing when I'm in my own *kitchen*. And when I *am* with him in the kitchen, which is at the rear of the house, and I can hear no car at all out in the front street, he might say something like "there goes Mrs. Cook."

"It might be *Mister* Cook," I say.

"No," he says. "Mr. Cook doesn't drive like that." Not just a certain car, but *who is driving it.*

***

If you ask him how many things he can hear at any one time, it is a great list. He told me once that one of my neighbours *three doors down* was having a pee! Something I did not particularly want to know, but I was intrigued.

"Are you sure?"

"Yes. In the water. Listen."

***

Bobbo loves me to read to him. The ritual started when we were at Bull Run and I used to read from books to our own kids at night; Bobbo would come over from their cottage and sit on Nick's bed.

When I moved here after Liz died our reading tradition was re-established, but after he saw me writing – and he would watch me do that endlessly – he wanted me to read only those pieces – usually things for the Gazette.

Red and Smithy are always with us during a reading session of course. They sit motionless with their heads in his lap, Bobbo stroking their ears – an audience of three. When I am finished, Bobbo continues to fondle them and is silent.

What does he get from a reading I have often wondered? It is probably something that I will never know. I am sure that sometimes I use words he cannot know the meaning of but he never asks. Does he picture a scene I describe? Or is it just the *act of my reading itself* that he finds comforting and pleasing? Whatever it is, I am glad to continue to do it for this kind and strange young man. Boy man.

***

"Hugh!" Mary has apprehended me again; this time I have been plonked into a huge armchair in one of the lounges in her hotel. "That crow! He's not mine at all. He's Bobbo's!"

This does not surprise me.

"I was playing a CD while Bobbo was cleaning that chandelier. Beethoven piano bits. I heard the crow so I got the bag of meat and we went up to the gazebo. I asked Bobbo to stand back because I thought Russell might fly off. That's what I'm calling him – original isn't it.

80

I put a piece of meat on the rail and the evil creature walked along as usual and took it. I said what I told you once about his refusing to take it from my hand and Bobbo went "aark" and the thing flew to him and landed on his shoulder! It turns out he and Russell are mates at the railway station. Did you know about that?"

"I knew about *a* crow but I didn't know he was yours."

"Not mine any more. Or we share him. Except, Hugh, he just *takes food* from me; he acts as though Bobbo is his *brother*!"

"Poor Mary."

"Yes poor bloody Mary. No children, no husband and now no crow!"

She asks one of her girls to bring drinks.

"Oh – something I just remembered. When we went up on the roof Bobbo paused the CD – he knows how to do that – and when we came down he played the rest of it. The last track was 'Moonlight Sonata', and when it finished – and I'm sure he didn't know the title – he said that he loved the moon."

Extraordinary – but not from that boy.

ELEVEN

VISITORS

The phone rings. "Will you come down to our party?" Mary Carmody.

"Mary, it's eleven o'clock."

"Oh poor old Hugh. Making your Ovaltine as we speak?"

"Well no, Nick is here. He came up from Brisbane with a friend. But I thought you said the Duchess just wanted women?"

"Yes, well, we've had a rethink. It's been lots of fun but we now think a couple of men would be alright."

"Very kind. Anyhow...*fun*? You've got a Royal Highness there."

"Hugh, I've told you before, she's – we're friends. She's very normal."

I am not tired as it happens. My son Nicholas and his flatmate Haydon and I have been talking non-stop and it has been great; we parents just do not see enough of our kids after they leave home, do we? Mary extends the invitation to my visitors.

***

I think there would be very few other Australian women who would be on such easy terms with a member of the British Royal Family. Their friendship began ten years ago, when the Duchess first visited the district. It had been the first overseas tour that the woman had made, and without her husband, who was unwell, and she had proved very popular. After that she had done most of her travelling abroad without the Duke; he died two years ago.

**

On the first day of that visit Mary told me there had been a big afternoon reception at the Civic Centre. Mary attended, and was talking with the Duchess at the very time that the visitor was scheduled to depart.

"I know that some people have come a long way and perhaps I haven't met everyone yet." The woman had said it more as a question, and to Roley Ziggenbine, Shire Chairman at the time and host for the occasion. A mistake; Roley needs only the smallest excuse to keep drinking at any time. As it was, Mary told me, he was beginning to get the smirk on his face that we have all come to know – the one that says his mental processes are starting to shut down.

"I can vouch that you have met everyone ma'am."

**

As the Duchess was leaving, her lady-in-waiting came over to Mary. "Her Highness understands that you walked here from the hotel and she asks if you would accept a lift."

"Thank you. Please tell her that our town is very pleasant at this time of day and I invite her to walk back with me."

And that is what they did, walking the twilight streets of our country town. As the visitor seemed to be enjoying it, Mary took many detours, so that the journey took nearly an hour. The Duchess was interested in flora and Mary identified for her our trees and shrubs, many of which were in flower: Bougainvillea, Bauhinia, African Tulip, Honeysuckle, Grevillea, Bottlebrush, Jasmine.....

"It could have been just Elsie Chatham and me on one of our regular strolls" – except for the pair walking fifteen paces behind, the lady-in-waiting and a policeman.

They had talked of everything and nothing, Mary said, and she sensed that the other was glad not to have to 'perform'. Mary told her something of our town's history – and she knows it better than most – and as they passed this house or that, she talked about its residents. Kids dashed about on bikes in the fading light, showing off.

Mary picked sprays of Bougainvillea and Jasmine. "I'll put these on your table." The Duchess was herself in the act of breaking off a stem of Bottlebrush when a boy called out from a now almost dark verandah. "Hey Mum, someone's pinching our flowers!" and the two women had scuttled on. When they did finally arrive at the hotel and the Duchess thanked them all, Constable O'Toole offered a red rose.

That night Mary was invited to the Royal's suite. It had been a warm day in early spring, and even at ten the temperature was mild, so they had sat out on the open first floor verandah. The woman had talked about her family and her life, and had been, Mary told me, extremely candid.

Mary took her to her own apartment and made up some cocoa while the woman looked at her books and pictures. They had gone up the little circular iron staircase to the tower and its gazebo and had drunk their cocoa looking out over the town.

***

The Duchess was scheduled to spend two days and nights in Redspear, an unusually long visit by a 'celebrity', but as she was coming straight from having flown into Brisbane, she had asked for a little extra time to overcome any jet lag.

Even so the woman had quite a busy program – opening the dam and the cotton gin, going through the new mine and presenting prizes at the Show and visiting district schools – but she and Mary were able to spend the last part of both evenings together.

When she left, the Duchess had invited Mary to come and stay with her, but on the two occasions since that Mary had visited England, the other woman had been out of the country.

***

I don't know just what we expect to see this evening – a group of women sitting and talking I suppose. What we do come upon is a sort of blind woman's bluff. 'It' is the Duchess, and the blindfolded Royal is groping out at a laughing, jinking circle of women.

Just after the boys and I arrive the Duchess touches Vera Scanlon's shoulder. It seems the rules are that Vera now has to stand still while her assailant attempts to identify her. This is almost more than Vera can take; she puts her hand over her mouth and twitches under the questing fingers.

"Vera," says the Duchess and removes her mask. She and Vera laugh and hug and then the Duchess pirouettes and sees us. One hand goes to her hair and the other smoothes her dress but she smiles through it all.

***

"Men are so conservative," says the Duchess in response to something I have said, as the two of us sip champagne and orange juice. She comes down on the "are", as if this had already been decided earlier by the women.

"I don't know that I am."

86

"No, perhaps you are not. Mary is very fond of you, you know."

"Yes I do. Can't think why."

"Well, everyone needs friends. But you're in business together too?"

"Yes. We have a motel on the other side of town."

"Business can be hard on a friendship......"

"True. It can ruin it. But we manage well. I don't know – maybe the age difference....."

"Perhaps...." She looks as if she might not continue, then "perhaps – you're the son....?"

"Yep. Could be. The son – or the husband she never had. Something."

***

"You know she's had good conversations, one on one, with all six of us," Mary tells me. "I didn't notice it 'til a little while ago. They're well trained but I think she's a natural."

"She doesn't stand on ceremony."

"No. She insists I call her Louise when we're on our own. She's good value. I think we'd have become mates if she'd lived around here.

When the Duke died there was a possibility she might have retired – dropped off The List. She's not a Royal by birth you know – her father was a farmer in Leicestershire. Still is. But she said they asked her to stay on. She said she was not fussed either way, even thinking of doing more study. She's got an arts degree and she's keen on anthropology. She wants to spend more time with her family too. There are several grandchildren.

Apparently the Queen rang and *came over* and more or less ordered her to stay with the Firm. I know why. She's very popular in England."

A thought strikes me. "Isn't there a lady-in-waiting somewhere?"

"Back in Brisbane; she's seeing relatives there. Louise asked if I would second one of my girls to be on hand and Vera volunteered. She's loving it." Vera is Mary's housekeeper at the hotel.

I look across at the visitor who is at this moment talking with my own guest, my son's friend Haydon. Whatever the subject is they are enjoying it. It could be a mother in conversation with her son – a polite, well brought up son, head bent towards the woman, nodding occasionally, smiling and attentive. He says something – seems to be describing something, using his hands. They both laugh, and she touches his arm.

*****

My son Nicholas tries to arrange one of his visits home each year to coincide with our three day Show. I was feeding my dogs in their kennels down behind the house just on dark two days ago when his Peugeot pulled up, and by the time I came around to the front he and Haydon were walking up the path. Nick kissed me – he still does that – and Haydon gave me a hug.

Though it was not cold I had lit a fire in the lounge room, as a welcome, and now I put out an early meal on platters, some spinach rolls and a pot of pea and ham soup and fresh bread and butter; the food disappeared in quick order. At one point Nick looked at me. "We'd better keep something for Bobbo."

Somehow Bobbo always knows when Nick is back in town, and sure enough a few minutes later there was a knock on the front door, and Nick took a plate of food out and the two friends sat together at my little table on the corner of the verandah.

***

My visitors stayed home that first night and I got to know Nick's friend a bit better. I had met Haydon before in Brisbane, when Nick and a girlfriend had taken me out to dine, and he had joined us at the restaurant later. I knew he worked in graphic design, like Nick – mostly with computers – and that his main job was creating Internet sites. He seemed to have a lot of work and I got the impression he was very well paid.

Both boys are knowledgeable about current affairs, with their own opinions, and au fait with what you might call the issues of the day. Very liberal, as you might imagine, and completely unracist and unsexist. However I came to realise during that first meeting with Haydon that he was quite ignorant about Queensland farming matters. He hadn't known about our tropical Bos Indicus cattle, and said he had not heard about Brigalow, the tree which had once covered huge swathes of this part of the state; he found it hard to grasp the place in our world of a stock and station agency such as mine.

I had some ripe cotton bolls in my car and when I showed them to him back at their flat he not only didn't know what they were but also had trouble associating the odd looking things with the shirt he was wearing.

I wondered if I wasn't as ignorant about *his* field. Certainly when he and Nick drop into computer-speak between themselves I cannot follow, but it's more the *jargon* that throws me; when they use everyday terms I manage.

***

As I am on the Show committee, the three days of their visit were hectic for me, and I really only saw the boys now and then, late in the night or in the early mornings.

We had a table at the Show Ball on the Saturday night. My son
Ralph and his wife Sally came in from our cattle property. I danced
with my daughter-in-law and whoever else would have me and my
two guests danced with just about every woman there. Once again
I saw how popular Nick is; whenever he walked to or from the bar
people greeted him, and it gladdened my heart to see the warm way
in which he responded. Anyone close to Nick has to share him with
a lot of people.

***

Haydon came into the kitchen early the first morning while I was
making tea and I got out an extra cup for him. He was wearing a
T-shirt and satin boxer shorts and I noticed – as anyone would – that
the lad had an erection, what people of my generation used to refer
to as a Morning Glory. I still get them, if I am bursting to urinate.

"If you're cold at all I can lend you a gown." Cover up man.

"I'll take you up on that Mr. Watson."

I went up the hall to my room but when I came back, the kitchen
was empty. I heard the toilet flush and a little later Haydon walked
back in. The thing had subsided but I gave him the dressing gown
anyhow.

I made a cup for Nick, put it on a tray with my own, and went to
his bedroom, Haydon following. It is a very big double bed in that
room and Nick pulled the blankets back and said "keep warm
Dad". I got in and Haydon handed us our cups and sat on a chair. I
moved to the centre of the bed, pulled back the blankets on my side,
and Haydon got in too.

So there we were, three grown men in the one bed – a scandal in the
making for Redspear. We talked for hours.

***

Now they are leaving. Their 'plan' was to depart by eight, which would have got them to Brisbane before dark, but it is now nine. It looked as if they might have been ready half an hour ago but Bobbo turned up again and Nick had gone to sit out on the back steps with him.

I am always curious to know what they talk *about*; from my experience Bobbo does not talk that much. While I was walking past – on the way to my outside laundry – it was Nick talking, and about his life in Brisbane. My two dogs as usual had their heads in Bobbo's lap.

***

Haydon is waiting at the little table on the front verandah, his bag beside him, and I join him. I appreciate the opportunity to talk with him on his own.

The boy has a lively face, with blue eyes and longish dark blond hair. His face is angular rather than round, and expressive. When he is talking there is much going on there, eyes widening, lips smiling, his head and hands moving. This morning his whole upper body, as he sits here, is mobile and expressive. It is a good body too, wide shouldered and fit; he has told me that he swims a lot and goes to a gym.

"The city slickers are leaving you in peace."

"And I regret it. I've enjoyed your company. *And* I've introduced you to Royalty."

"She was nice. No barriers there." We sit silent for a moment, then he says, "I do wonder what you think of me."

What *do* I think of Haydon? What I *know* is that he went to a State School on the Gold Coast, where his family run a fishing store, and after a couple of years of helping his family, attended the design course in Brisbane where he'd met Nicholas. He had moved in with Nick, sharing the rent.

"Well, since you ask, I like you and I think I can trust you."

"*Trust* me?"

What do I mean? "To be a good friend to Nick. Loyal."

"You're curious about me though aren't you? I have felt that."

"Yes – I'm curious about everybody, you know that," but he smiles and shakes his head.

"More." He takes a breath. "Is it about sex?" I am about to say 'not at all', but he continues."You wonder if I'm hetero?"

Is that it? Perhaps it is.

"None of my business, Haydon."

"No, it's alright. I'm gay."

***

At nine-thirty they do go, after goodbyes and more hugs. I stand at the gate and watch 'til they reach the corner, when arms emerge from windows and wave again. And then – that familiar, empty feeling as I walk back up the path; who of us hasn't felt it after loved ones depart. I have found that in my case there is one way to pick myself up at such a time; I ring my daughter Julie and we talk for an hour.

***

At two Mary is on the phone. "Someone wants to have a word."

The next voice is unmistakably English. "Hello Hugh."

"Good afternoon ma'am."

"I am on the plane back to Brisbane in an hour but I wanted to thank you for joining our little party last night."

"Well, we enjoyed it too."

"I'm glad. I liked Nicholas and his friend. You know, that Haydon is so like my youngest. He is gay too."

***

Now it is ten o'clock and Haydon rings. "Home safe," he says. And in the background Nicholas shouts, "Goodnight Dad."

"Goodnight Mr. Watson. Thanks again."

"Pleasure. Goodnight Haydon."

May life be good to both of you. Life be *fair* will do.

TWELVE

CROWS

Mary and Bobbo share a pet crow and now I too have one; though they all look alike to me Bobbo tells me it is not theirs; I wonder if everyone in Redspear has one.

I know one can find crows everywhere in Australia but I sometimes think our town has more than its share of them. They were the first living things I saw when I arrived here, and today I seem to be always in sight or sound of at least one of them.

Mine 'serenades' me each morning – from the Poinciana just outside my bedroom window – with that quiet liquid warbling they do. And the point occurs to me now – does he *know* in which room I sleep?

When I work in the vegetable garden down the back he keeps me company, being rewarded for his kindness every now and then with a grub or a worm. And when I sit on my verandah he walks across the side lawn to a point just below me and 'talks' to me.

This is too much for my dogs, and they rush along and down the steps to 'get' him, but of course by the time they arrive he is safely up on a branch of the nearby Kensington Pride, whence he scolds them.

I always had a strong antipathy to these birds, from the time I used to help Dad at the saleyards when I was just a kid in our town in western Victoria. There are always crows around saleyards, where there is an ever present chance of a death, and these are the carrion eaters non pariel. It used to annoy me for some reason when I saw them feasting on a carcass, and I would chase them away. My annoyance became anger and disgust when I saw for the first time some of them attacking a ewe that was having a prolonged lambing.

That loathing remained during my time at Bull Run, and if anything, deepened; although crows are more cautious about attacking an ailing cow, it does happen. Any time I had a .22 with me and saw a crow I would try to shoot it, and I have to say I encouraged my kids to do the same. Illogical really: they are part of the natural world and have their place – some would say a valuable one, as they do clean up a lot of carcasses – but there you are.

***

Change of subject. For several months early last year I was experiencing spells of lassitude. I had put it down to increasing age, but there was also an occasional ache in my left leg – not sharp but dull, and not centred on any part of the leg, but general. I had never had 'growing pains' as a kid but I imagined they might have felt like that.

Most of my ailments and injuries seemed to fix themselves, but the combination of symptoms this time was worrying me and eventually I trotted along to my doctor.

Albert McGauran is *everybody's* doctor – he has been in Redspear for so long. I like him, and particularly because he has the same aversion to putting drugs and antibiotics into the human body as I have. It is not as if he doesn't keep up-to-date though; he would be in his late seventies now but I find he is very sharp. Any time I mention some discovery or new technique I have heard of he seems to know all about it.

I have the greatest respect for his ability and experience – and so when he frowned after examining me I felt some alarm. He said he wanted me to go and see a specialist in Brisbane and right then he rang and arranged an appointment for later in the week.

"It could be nothing Hugh but if it isn't – well, we'd want to know wouldn't we?"

"Yes. You mean cancer?"

He raised his hands. "Possibly. Just possibly. It could also be some temporary thing. Reichel will do all the tests." He gave me a small bottle of syrupy-looking substance. "Take a teaspoon of this if you find you can't sleep. I use it occasionally. It's very mild."

***

Instead of driving to Brisbane by the south road, which goes right past my daughter's place, I decided to take the one that heads east first; I was gloomy, and felt that I wanted time on my own. It was an overcast day; a front had moved in and brought heavy cloud – a grey day to match my mood.

About fifty kilometres before the coast on this road there is a turning onto another that cuts across to join the highway south. At a motel on the edge of a small town on that road I called a halt. The owners prepared me a meal – I was the only guest – and I ate in my room and went to bed early.

I woke at three; a willy-wagtail was singing just outside my room. The cloud front had passed and there was now a clear sky with a bright moon. The little bird was singing his heart out, the way they sometimes seem to like to do on such nights.

I made a cup of tea, read for a while and then put out the light. The wagtail kept singing – he sounded very loud on that still moonlit night – and I thought I would only get to sleep if I chased him away, so I got up, went out, and shooed him off the rail of the porch. He flew only as far as a nearby bottlebrush, where he started up again.

I went out onto the lawn and shook the tree, but he moved no further than the next bush. I had to chivvy and chase that bird right along the side of the motel and around the back before he flew away.

My feet were freezing. There were cows grazing in the paddock next to the motel and they lifted their heads to watch me; I must have looked ridiculous.

I could not get back to sleep though, so just before dawn I decided to take off again, which meant I was in Brisbane quite early. I met up with Nicholas at a city café mid-morning; I did not eat or drink – not supposed to just before the blood tests – but it was good just to sit with my youngest.

"What's with this scan Dad?"

"An aching leg, on and off."

He gave me a searching look, frowning; I felt lapped by love. "Did you hurt it?"

"Well, I did get kicked a few months ago in the yards."

"Not one of those old Eureka Brahmans?"

"As a matter of fact it was."

"One got me out at Big Dingo!" he laughed; Nick has a great laugh.

***

I went to the specialist and gave blood and was prodded and pulled about in a thorough way, then made to drink a blue fluid and asked to come back in an hour and a half for the scan. I took myself to Queen Street Mall and bought a magazine and settled into a sunny spot but I didn't read much because I found too much interest in watching people. They seemed to me to be bursting with energy and self-confidence, while I felt old and vulnerable; I was about to do a test which I knew *might* reveal a medical condition which would alter my life – perhaps even signal its end.

I saw Nick walking up the other side of the Mall, a folder in his hand. He strode out, hair shining like a halo when he walked through a patch of sun. I didn't call out, content to watch him......

***

Waiting for the results back in Redspear was hard, but on the third day McGauran rang, and with good news. Nothing in my blood to worry about he said, iron a bit low and he would give me something for that. And nothing showing up in the scan on my leg.

I rang Nick and the other kids and was on a real high for the next twenty-four hours. *Only* twenty-four hours. McGauran rang again; there'd been another call from Brisbane – an 'anomaly' in the B test. They needed me to send another blood sample.

I did this – and went through the next three days like a zombie; I still made decisions at the agency, still talked with Errol at the motel, and even read letters at the Gazette, but I was only half with it. I could not get to sleep at night, not even with McGauran's syrup, which I suspected was a placebo.

That behaviour seems strange to me now, looking back. I am not a person who gives way to his fears or goes around feeling sorry for himself, but I acted then like a baby. I should have talked about it with the kids, or a friend like Mary, but instead I withdrew into myself. I think that I could have been reliving the breast cancer thing that took the life of my wife – that is all I can put it down to.

In the late afternoon of the third day I phoned the specialist myself. The nurse receptionist said he was busy with another patient and she asked me to hold on.

"Can you tell the result of that blood test?" I asked.

"No I can't do that but Dr. Reichel will be only a few moments and he...."

I interrupted; I had remembered her name. "Ruth, can't you at least tell me if it's okay?" There was a pause and fear gripped me but almost immediately Reichel came on – and gave me the all clear.

"Really, it was our equipment. We're going to have to check it all. Probably a good thing." A bloody good thing I thought.

***

Soon after that the leg ceased its ache and there was no more tiredness. Like all my previous ailments, they fixed themselves. I was back to my usual healthy self.

It *is* true though that you don't appreciate the things you have until you lose them, or in my case, imagine you might be *about* to lose them. Now I find I treasure my offspring and my friends more. I take every opportunity to phone them and to see them. I look for more ways I can help them.

I appreciate much more the physical world too. I feel strongly each change in the weather. I hear the *sounds* of nature more keenly, and delight in them, bird calls particularly, and yes, even those of my crow.

***

With my dogs now back at my feet on the verandah he has decided it's safe to come down again onto the lawn, but once again they get up to chase him; I do not call them off – they love me and are, as they see it, protecting me and mine. And my crow does not much seem to mind; they are part of his world, and he can handle them.

He flies up into the mango again, and begins to go through his repertoire which, if you have not spent time listening to crows, could surprise you. Squawks, mutters, gurgles and eventually songs come from the tree – and I am his appreciative audience.

He wants to be my friend; so be it, I shall be his.

THIRTEEN

MORE TREASURES

As I approach Rockhole Rest Area on my way back to town after a day at Bull Run, I notice activity there and I slow. I see a Council utility and then Neville Pitt cleaning some leaves off the top of the water tank; his wife Georgia is on the little slasher, cutting the grass around the toilets. I toot, but they do not hear because those machines are so noisy; Georgia sees me and waves.

Meet another friend – and this is an extraordinary one – able to master any job, solve any problem, manage any crisis. And all in a commonsense way, without fuss or drama. She is, I think, just the sort of person our country needs as a prime minister; she, with her mother Kitty as Treasurer, could not be bettered. Add their old friend Isobel as Governor General and we would have the perfect trifecta – The Kent Downs Gang.

***

"Kent Downs" was the first pastoral holding taken up in this area in the mid 1800's, and it was huge – as big as a European country. It is still very big – though carved up by governments over the years to make way for closer settlement. Our own Bull Run was originally part of it – just one of its enormous paddocks back then.

'KD' as we know it here was originally English owned, first by a titled family and then from about 1890 by an investing company, but the resident manager was always an Australian. It did not pass into Australian *ownership* until late in the twentieth century – to one of our big pastoral companies.

It has an enormous homestead. It was built in 1900, just after the years of the shearing strikes and during what was probably the worst drought since the arrival of Cook, and I am amazed that they could have contemplated constructing such a mansion at that time. I have been a visitor there many times and have always been awed by its size – two hundred squares at least. The rooms have four metre high ceilings, the hallway must be five metres wide and the verandahs six.

At the time it was built there was quite a settlement around it – at least twenty houses, and a dormitory for single men and itinerants, dozens of sheds and stables and a schoolhouse. Records show there were over a hundred people living there.

KD became very much the district's social centre, with balls, race meetings, tennis tournaments and parties. Premiers and Governors visited, and titled folk from England. As was the custom in newly settled areas of Queensland, *any* visitor was invited to stay, his accommodation ranging from a bedroom in the homestead to a bed in the men's quarters, depending on his status.

This 'settlement' was situated at the top end of a waterhole on the Ferguson River. At the bottom end of it, a good kilometre downstream, was the Aboriginals' camp. Apparently there were up to two hundred there at times.

A journalist who visited in the early 1900's wrote that the manager, H.K. Carter, was "very kind to the natives. He employs men as stockmen and gardeners, and girls and women as domestic servants. He feeds them very well, and even insists that any of the sick see the visiting doctor."

There was of course though a great social divide between black and white. Whilst the black children did attend school with the white children, the adults did not mix; no black people would ever have been invited to parties or dinners. (And I doubt if 'land rights' would have been a subject at any of those dinner parties.)

There was one kind of mixing. Many young white stockmen had liaisons with black women, and from the late 1800's onwards most of the children born there were of mixed blood. Almost none of these children were acknowledged by their white fathers; no white men ever met openly with Aboriginal women, certainly around the homestead, and any public displays of affection were unthinkable.

***

A girl whom the manager's wife named Kitty was born in 1917. (It was a common practice at that time for the "missus" to name the children born to Aboriginal women.) The father, a white stockman, moved on shortly after she was born, and the child never met him.

Kitty attended the school and, when she was old enough, began to work at the big house for Isobel and Jonathan Carter – "JS" – the man having 'inherited' the manager's position from his father.

Isobel Carter would tell me years later that Kitty was a quick learner and a good worker, and by the age of fifteen was doing all her work virtually unsupervised. She was given her own quarters in a hut at the rear of the homestead's gardens.

She had many boyfriends, amongst the succession of overseers and head stockmen, but she did not marry, or live with any of them. She did not have any children during this time.

***

In the mid 1940's a young Russian jumped ship in Melbourne. He travelled throughout the country, avoiding the authorities and getting work as a handyman, and gradually making his way north. He arrived at KD in 1950, and the Carters managed to get him citizenship. He and Kitty were married by a travelling clergyman the next year and exactly nine months later Georgia – our Rest Area tidier – was born.

***

That girl grew up learning all the station things that kids did then. She has told me she could ride almost as soon as she could walk, and did a year out in stock camps before even starting school. Outside of school hours she helped her father with the hundred and one things a handyman has to do on such a place, from carpentry to plumbing to greasing a car. She also helped her mother at the big house.

"Georgia was even more remarkable than her mother," Isobel Carter told me. "I don't think I ever had to actually *show her* how to do anything. She seemed to just *know*. By observation I suppose. She did everything confidently – in a proprietary way – as if the place were her own. Not just in the house, but the garden too, and it was a big one. I can still see her, just a slip of a girl, bossing her "uncles" around. They didn't seem to mind though."

"What was she actually employed as?"

"Just a housemaid really – for cleaning, washing, ironing, that kind of thing – and there was plenty to do; we had fifteen bedrooms and they were frequently all occupied. But if I needed help with anything else I would always get Georgia. Even with the cooking.

I remember once I went to thank the cook for some special thing that had been made for lunch – we had had important visitors – and there was Georgia, alone, washing up. Apparently the cook had been taken ill and Georgia had stepped in and done everything; she couldn't have been more than fourteen!

She was very good at her school work too and was a keen reader. She used to read a book while she was peeling potatoes. We let her use books from our library, and there was always one of them propped open somewhere. She loved Dickens.

She learned from her mother how to draw up the list of supplies we needed for the house, and for the store. It was an enormous list too; supplies had to last us for several months. It got to where I used to ask *her* what we needed; she was always ahead of me.

On top of all that though, she was a real tomboy. If she heard that her grandmother was going up river – fishing – she *had* to go. Sometimes they went into those hills to the east too, hunting goanna and echidna and wallaby and collecting bush tucker. She might be gone for a week then and this was difficult for me because I depended so much on her. I could never refuse her though; Jonathan used to grumble, but he loved to listen to all her stories when she came back."

***

In the 1960's Neville Pitt was living in Brisbane; he was not happy at home, and without much of a plan one day caught a train heading north out of the city; he ended up at Kent Downs.

He was a skinny kid, without any skills – he could not even ride a horse – but was lucky that the big stations at that time were short of staff, and were taking on almost anyone.

Georgia, the same age as the boy, took him under her wing. Within a couple of years he had become a competent stockman; they got married in 1971, when both were nineteen.

***

The first time I met Georgia was in the mid 70's. Liz's father had died and we had inherited Bull Run. We were facing our first big branding muster and two of our ringers had left and we were very understaffed. I asked Liz what her father would do in the same situation.

"Get Georgia and Neville from KD."

I had seen the pair once or twice at district do's. I recalled a lean, strong young man and a trim dark-haired young woman. I knew

105

she was part Aboriginal, and I thought I could see some evidence of that (but if I had not known I doubt if I would have thought it.)

"It will be full on for a week. Could she handle that?"

Liz gave me what used to be called an old-fashioned look. "You just try to keep up."

Well, the couple were eye openers. They did the work as if they had been *running* our place for years. Up before the rest of us – paddocks mustered before the heat of the day – fast and skilful in the yards with drafting and branding.

Neville had all the practical skills one would expect of a stockman but so had Georgia. And she could spy out a group of cows and calves half-hidden in timber before the rest of us. She had an intuition too – she always seemed to know where we would find the mob at any time of the day, in the largest paddock.

In the yards we used to put a station brand on all our calves of course but, on the females, individual numbers too. A heifer calf would barely be thrown but Georgia would have the next group of numbers ready, handing them to the brander in the correct sequence.

Neville and Georgia had brought not only their own little truck and horses but their swags too. I had planned that the rest of us would go back to the homestead after each day's work but she suggested we bring out our own camping gear and stay at whichever set of yards we were using at the time. I knew that would definitely be more efficient and that we would get the work done more quickly but we did not have a camp cook and I felt I could not spare one of us to do that job. "No worries," said Georgia, and worked even longer hours. Somehow she turned out stews and roasts and made bread; we even had puddings. We helped out by fetching firewood and peeling spuds and that sort of thing but she did most of it; she was a marvel.

When they were leaving I said, "I don't want you to go!" I had evil thoughts of poaching them – but I knew that even if I more than matched the pay they were receiving, they would not have come; KD was their home.

***

In the twenty odd years Liz and I had together on Bull Run, Neville and Georgia worked with us often. We reduced our staff and re-organised the work so that we did the big jobs only when they could come over. I used to worry each time about whether the manager of KD would agree to release them but he always did; I suppose I did not realise just how favoured a position Georgia had there.

Once when we decided to have a big party and ask the whole neighbourhood, I suggested to Liz that we have it catered. She said no, Georgia and she would do it. The woman came over two days beforehand and the pair produced an absolute banquet. I saw things I had never seen Liz make, and she confirmed they were Georgia's. (Years later, when I was eating at what was reckoned to be one of the best smorgasbord restaurants in Brisbane, my mind went back to that feast. "Almost as good as Georgia's," I said – aloud – to the bemusement of my fellow diners.)

It is worth repeating – *that woman could do anything*. If you needed a musterer, even in timbered country, there was none more adept or game than Georgia. She could build a fence; she could drive a semi-trailer; she was the best camp cook you could imagine.

And back at KD she and her mother looked after the district's grandest homestead. They would have made perfect hostesses at that homestead – if circumstances had been different.

***

Georgia was very good with children. Actually, they were very good with *her*; I think they recognised a superior being! But having her *own* children was one thing she could not manage; it seemed to be

107

common knowledge though that it was Neville's sperm that was the problem.

***

The couple lived and worked on KD for almost forty years after they were married. Neville became head stockman and then, shortly after the Australian company bought it, overseer. With the new ownership came a new manager, and Jonathan and Isobel Carter retired to Brisbane. Though the new manager had a capable wife, that woman wisely left the practical domestic details of KD to Georgia.

***

About ten years after the Australian takeover, the new owners organised a big reunion of KD employees to celebrate the sesquicentenary of its founding. All the neighbours were invited too; it became probably the biggest gathering of its kind ever held in Queensland.

It took place in October. Liz and I wandered the immense homestead gardens and met many old acquaintances, but it was a hot day and by midday we sought the shade of the homestead's wide verandah. Isobel Carter was there, on an upholstered cane sofa which had been put there especially for her.

She was in her eighties by then but looked well. She looked happy too, with Kitty on one side of her on the sofa and Georgia on the other. Aboriginal mother and daughter sat with her all afternoon; I noticed that for much of the time they held Isobel's hands.

***

Ten years later again I was in Brisbane on business when I received a message from home; could I make time to go and see Isobel Carter?

When I arrived at Isobel's house, a big Queenslander in one of the old parts of Brisbane, I was met by a nurse. It was a cool winter's day but Isobel was on the verandah, propped up on a day bed in a sunny corner. She was thin and smaller.

"Hugh, my dear," she said, and opened her arms for a hug and a kiss. She expressed sadness for my loss and hoped I didn't mind talking about it.

I didn't, not with her, though Liz had been dead only six months. Isobel had known us for so long – Liz all her life and me since I was in my twenties – that she was like an old and loved aunt.

I talked about life at Bull Run and how I was planning to move into town. She asked about people she had known, which was just about everyone in our district. She seemed to be very up-to-date and I said so.

"Georgia writes to me often. That's one of her letters there," pointing at the little side table.

"You were always a good friend to her," I said.

She nodded. "And her mother."

"Yes. I remember when they had that big reunion at KD. You sat with those two for hours. You all looked so happy."

"They are my family," she said – and then she told me so much more.

***

"When Kitty began coming up to the house to do domestic work, she was about ten years of age, the same age as our boy Andrew. They were already friends; they used to sit next to each other in class, and Andrew used to go with her and her family when they went fishing or hunting.

Kitty you know had a full blood mother and had lived down in the camp up to then but she fitted in so easily with us. Her father had been an uneducated stockman and as I remember not very bright, but she was clever and she wanted to learn. Very observant, very

109

quick. And her manners were a delight. I used to say to Andrew, "if you want to know the proper way to act, watch Kitty."

Those two spent all their spare time in each other's company. They grew up as mates and – well – you're probably ahead of me, they fell in love.

I noticed how strong the attraction was long before Jonathan did. We women have this thing called intuition you know Hugh. But eventually I gave Jonathan a hint and he saw it himself. And of course he had to *do* something."

She stopped and turned her head. She looked down the length of her verandah and her mind drifted. I think she was going back those fifty years – perhaps looking down that other longer and wider verandah. Her voice, when she started again, had a different tone.

"Hugh, it was not possible. At that time, no white family in our position would have accepted an Aboriginal daughter-in-law. We – my husband anyhow – could not countenance it." Her voice trembled.

"But *you* would not have had any objection?"

Her face turned to mine, sharp, her eyes bright. "She was a wonderful girl. She would have made a perfect wife for him. Even – even if they'd had to leave ... "

"Would they?"

"Yes, I am sure of it. Andrew had his heart set on taking over at Kent one day and we already knew that the owners in England were agreeable. But somehow someone said something in England and we got a letter from the Chairman. He said that if Andrew married 'the half caste girl' then he could not be considered for the position. 'Regrettably'. Some reason of 'proper governance' was given. It was just prejudice really. 'Regrettably' – I remember the word. It says a lot but says nothing." She made a dismissive gesture.

"Jonathan had his heart set on Andrew taking over but he said we'd have to send him away for a while – a long tour to the company's other properties around the world. 'It will do him good – he'll learn a lot'.

I know he was hoping that Andrew might fall for some other girl somewhere. I didn't give that much chance; he and Georgia were so attached. But I agreed – Andrew accepted the offer – and off he went. Forever."

Isobel's bony hand had clutched mine as she said this and now she stopped speaking and began to tremble. I did not need to ask what had happened; the whole district knew the story of how Andrew had died in a shooting accident on one of the company's ranches in Brazil. We sat silent for several minutes, then she sighed and 'came back'.

"So you see Hugh I lost my son, and for what? Nothing! Nothing! All I had then was Kitty. My Kitty. We grieved together – and she stayed with me. I know there were boyfriends – goodness knows she had many opportunities to leave – but she stayed for ten years. She was *caring* for me, and I loved her for that.

I never encouraged any of her relationships and that was selfish of me; for some reason though when Alexei came along I thought 'enough'. I showed Alexei I liked him and told Kitty I did. For the first time I 'let go'. So they were married and before you knew it, along came Georgia." She turned her face up to me with a smile. "They are my family. My daughter. My granddaughter."

***

Just two months after my visit to her home, Isobel Carter died. Georgia and Neville and Kitty and Alexei and I were part of a huge contingent who travelled down to Brisbane for the funeral; we sat together in the church.

***

Kitty and Alexei stayed at KD for another ten years in their 'grace and favour' cottage, then came in to Redspear. Alexei died two years afterwards, but Kitty is still with us.

In time Georgia and Neville moved here too, Neville finding he could no longer do his work because of stiffness in his joints and the general aches and pains resulting from countless falls and busters with horses over the years. He got this job with the Shire Council looking after our Rest Areas and Georgia sometimes goes out with him on his rounds; she also has a part-time position at the hotel with Mary.

***

Georgia is sixty now – a couple of years younger than I – but I think she can still do as much as two or even three women her age. I was at a civic reception recently and was tucking into the finger food provided by Carmody's when there was Georgia in front of me, smiling and offering a tray, trim in the black outfit all the 'girls' were wearing. Yet, quite likely, she had already spent most of the day helping to keep our district neat and tidy.

***

The toot of my horn as I pass Rockhole Rest Area is as much a salute as a greeting. To her and her mother and her 'grandmother'.

FOURTEEN

A SMALL MYSTERY

I have been 'summoned' to Mary's apartment – Georgia is there too – and it is not a social occasion. The three of us are staring at a sheet of paper on the little table in front of us. On it are the words that Georgia had copied from inside the Ladies' lavatory at one of the Shire's Rest Areas – Sandstone, on the highway eighty kilometres south of Redspear.

"They were in black – Texta I think – about a metre up the wall, close to the seat," Georgia says."I've copied them exactly."

It is obvious to me why she had gone to that trouble. H and C are in capitals and large, but the other letters are in lower case and quite small, in fact so small that any reader would have had to get very close to read them. When she had, she would have read 'Helen is a Cunt'. What she would have seen from some distance, and very clearly, was simply H C.

"Helen Carruthers," says Mary.

"It mightn't be," I say.

"No," then after a pause, "but I have a strong feeling that it is."
She says this slowly and emphasises the 'is'. "What do you think
Georgia?"

Georgia nods. "I don't know any other H C."

I continue to look at the words; they hold a fascination.

"I'm worried," Mary says. "We should talk to the police."

"It's not a crime, what this person's done," I say.

"I think it is. Libelling another person."

"Insulting 'H C' is not necessarily a libel of Helen Carruthers."

"The police might have heard something," says Mary, disregarding
my words. "Or they could talk to Helen and see if she's fallen out
with anyone lately."

"I don't think we should do anything. Or even worry about it. It's
just a few words on a wall," but I too feel fairly sure that it is our
Helen. Georgia excuses herself and goes back to her work in the
hotel.

On the table next to the writing pad is another sheet of paper with
the words, 'H C is a bitch' in the identical writing style. Georgia
had copied this earlier in the week from the amenities on Paradise
Creek, sixty kilometres to the east of town.

Two thoughts are going through my mind. One is the sheer
ridiculousness of it. Helen Carruthers! Respectable, courteous, a
good citizen – the last person one would expect to attract this sort of
thing.

The other thing is the style of writing itself; it is neat – rather old
fashioned – the letters very well formed, and finished almost with
fussiness. I point this out to Mary.

"Yes, it *is* unusual, isn't it. Actually it reminds me of the writing we
had to practise off our blackboard at school."

I know what she means; it is almost as if the lower case words had been written between parallel lines, the letters all exactly the same height.

I pull out my pen and try writing in the same style. The result is just a variation of my usual scrawl until I try to imagine a blackboard and begin moving my whole arm, not just my fingers. It comes then, and after a few attempts I have a reasonable copy of the graffiti, except that I can only do it by writing *big*. Whoever had done this had had sufficient control to write very small.

Mary takes my pen and also tries, achieving a good copy more quickly than I had. "Yes, it's like I used to learn at school."

We sit in silence a while. I say, "I'll talk to the Sergeant", because I know she wants me to do something. "Who knows about this?"

"You and me and Georgia."

"Not her husband?"

"No. And she won't tell Neville yet."

"OK. I suggest we keep this to ourselves." She nods. "When does Neville go round again?"

"Monday morning."

"Does Georgia always go with him?"

"No – some afternoons. Just to keep busy I think. She works here 'til twelve."

"Can you let her off next Monday morning?"

"Of course."

"Will Neville think it odd that his wife is free in the morning?"

Mary shakes her head.

***

I have been talking to Sergeant Hagan for only a minute before I am regretting the visit. I react badly to certain policemen; when faced with one who is heavy handed I tend to become 'difficult', and if one says something to me in a tone that is not to be questioned, I question. This sergeant is pushing those buttons; I have a strong feeling that he overly enjoys his power.

He asks me now if Georgia said she remembered a vehicle at either of the sites and I tell him no and then he asks me if I have any suspicions about anyone. Again, no.

"Are you saying you think everyone loves our Mrs. Carruthers?"

"Obviously someone doesn't, but it beats me. Helen is the last person you'd expect to attract this sort of thing." And then, because I don't like his tone, "wouldn't you say?"

He shrugs. "Oh well Mr. Watson, we've both been around a few years," giving me what I would call a knowing smile.

"Meaning ... ?"

"Oh – that we don't know everything about our friends. I would have thought a 'journalist' would agree with that?"

I am not agreeing with anything.

***

I have walked to the Police Station, and since it is at the river end of our main street and near Helen's motel, I have decided to do some sleuthing. I am now sitting with her under one of the huge Bauhinias there, and sipping a rum-and-lime.

***

This woman, as I know I have said, is a stunner, though there was a period – for ten years or so after her divorce – when she 'let herself go' somewhat, putting on weight, and seeming not to care much about her appearance. She seemed to take no interest in men and they did not seem to take much of an interest in her; I remember I

116

had the impression that she was living just for her two daughters and her work, first as a teacher then here at the motel. But about the time she and her business partner Mary expanded and renovated the motel, she renovated herself as well. She trimmed down, cut her hair, put on make-up and wore different clothes; the Siren re-emerged.

With the change has come a lot of increased interest from men, locals and visitors, but, so far as I know, not reciprocated.

***

Watch this Holmes, I think – 'Watson is on the case'.

"How are things here?"

"Fine. Running like clockwork."

"One of my cleaners took some money the other day." A little lie, for the purpose. "We had to sack her. Not pleasant is it?"

"I imagine. I never have any trouble like that, touch wood."

"No trouble with tradesmen?"

"No. I must be lucky." Not really: a smiling request from Helen would have any of the local tradesmen offering to do her jobs instantly – and for free.

I try another tack. "Errol says his biggest headache is the public: stealing blankets, messing up rooms, that sort of thing."

"Yes I do occasionally get some of that. Oh, there's the police car. I must catch the Sergeant if it's he."

I can see the car coming up the side road. Helen stands. "I've got an apology to make. He's asked me a few times to come to those 'Friends of the Police' gatherings he has down there and I've said I will, but every time something else has come up."

I say I have to go anyhow and begin my walk home. From a distance I notice that the police car has slowed but then picked up speed again, and Helen has begun to walk back to her office, and I assume it must have been one of our constables driving.

***

A fortnight or so later the graffiti thing has almost slipped from my consciousness, but Mary rings to say Georgia has found another.

In Mary's apartment again – our 'operations room' – we stare at the now familiar script. This time Mary has asked her manager Rob to be present too.

'H C Too good for you and me.'

"Are you sure it is new?" I ask Georgia.

"Yes. In the Ladies at Kelly's Waterhole."

"What do you make of it Rob? You've seen the earlier ones?"

He nods and frowns. "This one seems – bitter."

"Yes," says Mary. "Not like 'bitch' – or that other word. They were just *hard*. This is more – well – resentful. And you know I *can* see a local thinking that Helen gives herself airs. Someone who lacks confidence could think that."

"So – and I'm grasping here – if it *is* a woman – and just because it's in the Ladies doesn't mean it is – but *if* it is, could it be someone whose friendship has been rejected by Helen ...?"

"It could be unrequited love." We all look at Mary.

"Well, it happens. I know Queen Victoria didn't believe it was possible but I've seen plenty in this place you know."

"Or..." now Georgia, "it could be someone who knew her *bloke* had fallen for Helen but had been rejected..."

"That's deep," says Mary. "Helen's never told me about anything like that – but then she probably wouldn't."

"She mightn't *know*," says Georgia. "But say it has happened, and the wife knows – or suspects – then rejecting *him* is like rejecting *them*."

We digest this in silence.

Georgia went on. "Helen is saying the man might be good enough for you but not for me. And that could hurt."

Georgia looks to Mary for support and her employer nods.

"Well," I say, "it could be the *man*. Putting everyone off the track by writing in the Ladies." I look at Rob and *he* nods.

We nodders decide we will not tell Helen yet. If it recurs we will – but hopefully, we tell each other, this is the last. This message does have something of a feel of finality about it, and I certainly hope that is so. This has been a very disquieting thing – not at all *my Redspear*.

FIFTEEN

COMING TO TERMS

As I drove along our main street last week I saw an old woman walking from a parked Jaguar into the entrance of Carmody's Hotel. I recognised the car first – the only Jag that I know of in the district – and then its owner, Carinda Anderson.

Her entering Mary Carmody's place intrigued me because I know there is history between those two women. But if there were to be a meeting I thought I could guess the purpose; Mary lends loads of money and Carinda is known to be in financial difficulties.

Mary has not since told me if she and Carinda did meet that day, and if so what they talked about – and I suppose she won't; though the old busy-body tries to pry other people's secrets from them, she can be very close about some of her own dealings. The possibility of a meeting intrigued me though, enough to prompt me to write the following – something entirely from my over-active imagination.

***

The solicitor had phoned Mary the previous afternoon and said that his client would contact her directly, and her phone call came the next morning. Mary was in the dining room, having her daily conference with her manager and head girls; she walked back to her office at the rear of the hotel to take the call in private.

"If you are free this afternoon, Mr Ecclestone has offered us the use of an office," the woman said. "It's a nice little private room and I can make us some tea there if we wish."

Mary knew it; as she had multiplied her businesses and built up her fortune, she had come to know many such 'private rooms' in her town. "But I really need to be here. Some other things are happening."

"Oh, well, if today's not convenient....."

"No, each day this week is the same I'm afraid."

"I could come in on the weekend. I'm sure Mr Ecclestone wouldn't mind."

"The Premier's party is staying here then, and they want me too for some reason. No, this afternoon would be best." The woman, Mary thought, did not want to come to the hotel but *this* was where she preferred to do all her business now. She decided to close it off.

"Let's say 3 o'clock? In my office?" There was silence. "Mrs Anderson?"

"Yes. Very well. And please – it's Carinda."

***

"It's Carinda," her friend Ivy had said, in the burns hospital those many years before, as she replaced the boy's letter in its envelope. "She's been against you and Ferguson from the start."

Mary had sensed it and others had told her. Carinda Gibbs' family owned "Pennington", the only property in the district still retained by the descendants of the original settlers. The region's main rivers both ran through it, and the mother had named her two children after them. Carinda Gibbs acted as if the river had been named after *her*; hardly anyone would have been good enough to marry her brother.

"Well – a bar girl ..."

"Oh Mary you aren't a bar girl! Your father absolutely depends on you, and besides you'll probably own the place one day. Anyhow it's not that – well I suppose it is a bit – but no, it's really because she wants to get married first so she can make sure she gets her share of the property. She's frightened if someone gets their hooks into her brother she'll lose too much."

"I think the parents would be against me anyhow."

"Mildred might be but not Harry. It's Carinda you'll have to beat though."

But she knew she had already lost. The hotel fire that had taken her own mother's life had also seen to that. Even after a year of 'successful' operations and grafts she could still barely bring herself to look in a mirror. What hope of Ferguson – of any boy ......?

Ivy placed the envelope back in the drawer of the little cupboard beside the bed. "Ferguson's just saying goodbye for a bit. When he comes back from overseas you'll pick up just where you left off, you'll see."

***

It had not surprised Mary when her father decided to rebuild the old wooden hotel after the fire, but she hadn't dreamed he would do it on such a scale – two storeys high, in brick, and this time the full main street frontage. When he died eight years later the hotel became hers, along with a great deal of money. She discovered in the years that followed that she had a good head for business; she built up a great fortune – a fortune that now drew many people.

***

She decided not to have the meeting with Carinda in her office but on the first floor verandah next to her private apartment; her girls set up a little table and some chairs there. When her visitor was seated she herself sat so that she was in part profile, as she had learned to do long ago, the fire ravaged side of her face more or less out of view; she knew how upsetting it was to people who were unused to it. A girl brought the tea things – Shelley porcelain and sterling silver.

"Tea?"

She had done her homework; she hadn't made her money without doing that. Carinda and her husband had borrowed against Pennington after the last beef crash, when interest rates were high, and, though beef was now good again, income from the place was barely covering the annual repayments; a renegotiated loan at a lower interest rate was needed. It would be for quite a few hundred thousand dollars but the debt would be well covered by equity, the property being worth several million, and, Mary knew, unencumbered.

As for the personal – she believed she harboured no ill will towards Carinda Anderson nee Gibbs. That had all been a long time ago.

***

"I was sorry to hear about your husband," Mary said.

"Oh, Edward had been ill for years. It was a release really."

"Still – when people finally go …"

"He was a few years older than me you know," and then, as if to herself, "but that didn't make Edward a good manager, being older. We should have made decisions together." Mary opened her mouth to speak, but the other woman went on. "You've managed your own business affairs and everyone admires you for it. Of course you've never married."

Mary tensed. She could think of nothing to say but Carinda seemed to be on a track. "You knew my brother Ferguson died last year?"

She nodded. Heart attack in his house in Manningham. But what was the woman doing? They didn't need to go back.

"You were friends with him once weren't you?" Smiling, and now turning her head this way and that, as if seeking something to aid her memory. "I seem to remember one or two very nice evenings here."

***

Mary Carmody did not believe she was a vindictive woman, or unfair, but she knew she could be tough, and give as good as she got. She made a decision – she was not copping this – and like a battleship coming about she turned slowly in her chair until she was directly facing her visitor.

"Your father and I became friends too."

"Really? I didn't know that."

"Yes. We'd sit here in the evenings and talk – those times when he came into town and stayed for a couple of days. I think he was lonely."

"Oh no, it couldn't have been that. We were always there and..."

"He told me he wished Ferg and I had married. More cake?"

"No thank you. Um – did he?"

"Yes. I told him that at the time I was keen but do you know what he told me then? He said that I wouldn't have stood a chance because 'the women were against it'."

"Which women?"

"I assumed he meant you and your mother. More tea?"

"That's not right. I mean he wouldn't have – " Mary had picked up the teapot. "No thank you." Carinda took a deep breath and then tried a smile again. "Why would I have had anything against you?"

"Exactly. That's what I asked your father."

"And what – did he...?" She seemed unable to finish.

You asked for this Carinda she thought. I really don't care about all that any more but if you want to use my money, you'll have to know I won't play your games.

The other woman was looking anywhere but at her. Mary relented and turned back to her profile position but her guest now stood, and began to pick up her jacket and her handbag. Mary thought she heard a choked sob.

"Don't go Carinda."

The other woman remained standing, half turned away, her shoulders hunched. "It's true. I can see you know it. I shouldn't have come. You must hate me."

"I don't hate you. I think I did for a bit. But it wasn't you that turned Ferguson away, it was this," touching her face.

"But it would be natural if you did hate me. I feel as if you *should*."

"Well I don't. But I couldn't let you go on treating me like a dummy." The woman sagged back into the chair and Mary passed across a box of tissues. Carinda took one and wiped her eyes.

"Now," said Mary, "terms."

SIXTEEN

LOSING ROBBIE

"Look at the stars tonight," I said.

"I think it's because there's no dust," said Meg Cotter. "My grandmother used to say 'polished by the celestial winds'. Gran was given to expressions like that."

"I like 'written in the stars'," said Robbie.

"Sounds Middle Eastern, doesn't it."

"Yeah – the Three Wise Men....." My friend pushed his wheelchair closer to me and leaned his muscular arms on the rail of the verandah. "Actually Hugh," he said quietly, "I have my own star."

"Can you point it out?"

A burst of laughter made us look down onto the lawn. A couple of the girls were up on their partners' shoulders and the four were doing a ludicrous tango.

**

This was at the Cotter's last Saturday night, a twenty-first for their Madelaine. There were about fifty of us, youngies and parents. There was a disco thing, and the little wooden dance floor that had been set up outside was getting a good pounding. Every so often, when the rock numbers of our youth were being played, we oldies bullocked the others off and took over, but by midnight the youthful more or less had the floor to themselves, and the rest of us were drinking and yarning.

Robbie Riley and I were sitting with our hosts at a corner of their big open verandah. Now the Cotters excused themselves for some reason and went off to some other part of the house. I intended to ask Robbie to point out 'his' star but as he and I watched the energetic kids down on the dance floor my mind turned to wondering what my companion might have been thinking; he would never be able to leave his chair and do that. I looked over at him, discreetly I thought, but found him watching me.

"At least that's one way I'll never make a fool of myself." He seemed to have read my mind. No bitterness in his voice though.

It encouraged me to say "you're not missing much."

"Aren't I?" And then, the way some conversations suddenly do, this one went deeper. "Dancing is for mating. I don't know if I'll be mating."

It wasn't a moment for an 'of course you will one day' remark; I owed him better than that. Although I am more than twice his age, we have always managed to talk to each other in a straight way, like contemporaries. But what to say?

"Do you have...?" I was going to say 'sexual feelings' but I stopped myself; of course he did. 'Strong desires' I thought might be better – but baulked again – too Victorian.

Robbie rescued me. "I get horny." I smiled in gratitude. "What do I do about it?"

He cupped his hand and made the universal movement.

"Well we've all done that." Joe Cool. "Even married men."

He told me he got aroused easily and often. "Actually I think I may be naturally highly sexed. From my Dad I'd say. Anyhow I don't let it get to me. I jerk off and get on with life. Or work."

***

Getting on with work Robbie certainly has. Since he began employment with Mary Carmody seven or eight years ago he has, it seems to me, done the work of two or three men.

At the time he began with Mary she was already wealthy; inheriting that huge hotel from her father when she was just thirty had been an immensely helpful start but she had not let things rest there. She had overhauled each of the hotel's activities; the bars, the dining rooms, the accommodation were all expanded and modernised, and the little row of shops under one end of her verandah, which had been almost a liability, had been converted into an asset, with Helen's assistance.

All this had given her a bounteous flow of cash, and she invested in any local initiative that looked promising. People began to come to her for loans as well, and she acquired more assets when some of the loan repayments were not met. Her money made money, as it does.

When she asked Robbie to come and help her manage this conglomeration he was working for me, you may remember, and was just finishing his commerce degree. He was only twenty-one but it had become obvious to all of us that he was possessed of real business acumen.

Once he had got his head around her many business activities and investments he began to streamline them, and always with an eye to increasing the returns.

Mary used to talk about Robbie to me quite a lot in those first few years. She told me he was putting so many ideas to her that he made her head spin. After just two years she had so much confidence in him she told me she more or less let him have his head; at the same time she proposed a profit sharing arrangement with him.

They have invested in all the developments that have taken place in Redspear in the past few years, which are considerable. With irrigation, and with first one then two coal mines nearby, our town has jumped ahead; Mary has her fingers in many profitable pies. The woman talks in millions the way the rest of us talk in thousands. Robbie himself, still only twenty-eight, is now probably worth a million or two. But he does not have a mate.

***

After seeing him master every job at the Gazette as a very young and energetic protégé, and then learning how well he was doing with Mary, I had more or less ceased to worry about the young man. He had overcome obstacles so big, and was doing so well financially, I thought of him as an outstanding success. On top of that, he always projected optimism and cheerfulness – an energetic, capable and likeable young man.

But – none of our young women had, apparently, been attracted enough to become his partner. The thought makes me almost angry; had none bothered to look past the lopsided face and the wheelchair and those thin twisted legs? Had none appreciated his courage, his character, his intellect?

Yesterday in the main street I saw him and a young woman standing near his car; I recognised her as the Brewer girl. She had a sheaf of papers in her hand and I remembered that she does extra work on a word processor at home. Robbie was reading her work, balancing easily on one of his sticks as he scanned the pages.

The girl is young and pretty. Robbie made her laugh at something, but – and I think I can read body language – she seemed tense. Though she was almost a metre from the man there was a backward lean to her upper body. If he had reached over and touched her arm would she have flinched?

***

I was talking with his boss in the courtyard at the back of her hotel when Robbie came out of his office on the floor above. He sped down the ramp – *his* ramp – did a two-wheel turn at the bottom and came over.

"Robbie, we were just thinking of a drink."

"Can't, sorry. I'm going to the gym," as he removed his business shirt and reached around to a pocket at the rear of the chair and pulled out an old tee-shirt.

"Superman" we sometimes call Robbie. Yesterday, as he raised his arms to put on the shirt, the muscles in his chest and arms bunched and rippled. Bare-chested, Robbie Riley is a picture of almost overpowering health and fitness.

"See you," he said and took off for his car, but before he reached it he did another turn and came back. "What do you think of Rob?"

"What do you mean?" asked Mary.

"As my name? Instead of Robbie."

"What's wrong with Robbie?" I asked.

"It's – juvenile."

Mary chuckled. "At my age *everyone* is juvenile." But Robbie did not smile, so she said, "I suppose we could live with Rob, couldn't we Hugh?"

"Of course, but it'll be difficult for us. We've only ever known you as Robbie."

"Impossible for me I'd say," said Mary. "Stay juvenile."

Robbie – Rob – waved a fist in mock anger and sped away to his car. Mary and I stood in silence. I was thinking of saying something about our friend but she pre-empted it.

"Hugh, I think we are losing Robbie."

"Rob."

She smiled. "Well, that's part of it too," and she told me other things. She believed he was thinking of travelling overseas. Brochures on European and American cities were appearing on his desk, and envelopes with the names of well known overseas companies on them. "Sachs Goldman was one."

"What has he said?"

"Nothing yet, but he doesn't hide anything either. And he still manages my business very well. Very thorough. But there's a *perspective* about everything he says now. As if – well – this work has been just *part* of his life, this job and me and Redspear – and you." She sighed. "He'll tell us when he's ready."

We both stood silent a moment. A big dry seed pod from the Poinciana under which we were standing fell to the paving behind us with a loud rattle. We both jumped.

***

In fact he was about to tell. As I was watering the roses in my front garden later that day, I saw Rob's old Volvo coming up the street. It slowed down, and I turned off the hose and walked out the gate. Rob smiled at me through the open window.

"Just in time," he said, and pointed up. "There's my star Hugh."

I looked, but it was too early for stars. What I did see was the winking light of a high north travelling jet.

SEVENTEEN

AN INCIDENT

Mary rings to say that one of her cleaners, who lives opposite the sergeant's house, has told her that Mrs. Hagan has been taken away in an ambulance. She said that the ambulance officers were in the house a long time before they carried the woman out on a stretcher.

"Carrie says she thought she heard a shot earlier and she thinks that when Hagan came out of the house he seemed to have blood on his shirt."

"Are they up at the hospital?"

"No, well Mrs. Hagan is. The sergeant's back inside. Carrie went over to see if she could do anything but he said no."

"How did he seem?"

"She said he didn't come out. He spoke through the kitchen window."

An hour later she rings again. "Sorry if I am disturbing you. I rang the hospital; Mrs. Hagan isn't there. They've taken her to Manningham!"

***

A day or two later I happen to meet one of our constables in the street and he says the sergeant is being transferred to Manningham so he can be near his wife. "Mrs. Hagan's in a – a special – I'm not supposed to say any more Mr. Watson," but looks as if he would like to.

"Then don't Damian. Silence for a yes. A mental health place?" Silence. "There was talk of a shot being fired?" Silence. "There was blood?"

"Not hers," he blurts.

***

Though I do not like Sergeant Hagan I decide to call at his house to see if there is any help I can lend. And yes I admit, to satisfy some of my curiosity.

I find him packing things from his garage into a tea chest on his driveway. As I walk towards him I can see a neat bandage on his left hand around the thumb. Whether I am so obviously looking at it or because it is on his mind (it would at least have been making his packing a little awkward) he says, "damn thing – cut it the other night."

"I heard you were leaving?"

"Yes, time to move on." A pause, and I feel him picking his words. "My wife's not well and she'll need to spend some time at Manningham so it makes sense to go there. Would you like a drink?"

***

So for the first time I sit as a guest in the Hagan home. The lounge room, and so far as I can tell the whole house, is still furnished. It is very neat – no clutter on the bench top, no papers spilling off a table as in Chez Watson. Hagan – his name is Eric – says how much he's *liked* his time in Redspear. He is speaking without his usual edge, as

134

if he means it. "This is a good posting for someone. I'll be sorry to leave."

I know a little about his wife. There was a drink problem, and she did not mix much with the locals. I remember she came to the Winter Ball just after they arrived here three years ago but not again, and not to much else. She had the younger policemen and their wives or girlfriends over for a barbecue once a year, and she answered the phone if they rang after hours and her husband was not there, but that was all the contact people seemed to have had with her. According to Mary, constables on weekend duty at the station had heard shouting at the Hagan house.

***

"I don't envy you your job Eric. Having to learn all about us and our funny ways then bang, off to the next place."

"You get used to that."

"Perhaps you'll find a place you just won't want to leave?"

He nods. "Whether I want to stay or not, Manningham will be our last. With a bit of luck I'll make Inspector and that'll do."

"Any children Eric?"

"No. My wife – couldn't..."

"That's a shame."

"Oh I don't know. Mightn't have made much of a father." That is said somewhat flatly, but the next words are uttered almost angrily. "From what I've seen most people are lousy parents."

"We all fail a bit, that's for sure. Somehow some of us are rewarded with nice kids." But he is shaking his head, dismissively.

"There's hardly anyone in this town I'd call a decent parent."

There it is again, I think to myself; he doesn't really like his fellow man. He doesn't respect us either. I know of the hard times he has given people that he has picked up in town for minor offences; he used to frighten the younger ones with his questions and his manner, acting as if he would like to lock them up and throw away the key. An unhappy man.

I finish my drink and say I have to go. We shake hands; he has big hands and his grip is very strong. I see dried blood on the bandage. I wish him well, but I do not say I hope we will meet again.

EIGHTEEN

TEAMWORK

A Saturday morning and Mary, Helen and I are headed for
Manningham on the coast for the regional final of the competition.
The four hour trip in my Landcruiser is passing quickly. We are
enjoying ourselves, talking and playing riddles and even singing –
but I know we have a real fight ahead.

Once I had learned who we were up against I had phoned the
editor of the paper at Dargan. Claude Simpson said 'Delta' had been
streets ahead of the other teams in their local knockout. "They're
good, don't you worry about that," (as a certain Queensland
politician used to say.) "They smile a lot. One even knitted all
night. They're a bit unnerving." I had warned Mary about these
barracudas. "Bring them on," the eighty-eight year old had said.

***

The three quiz rounds are to take place in the 'Learmonth', a
big new theatre named after a former long-serving mayor of
Manningham. We arrive before the other teams and a full hour
before the first round is due to start, but the hall is already half full.
We are taken backstage and given a dressing room that we are told
we will be sharing with our rivals; it is large, furnished with an

open-fronted wardrobe, armchairs and some small tables. There is a fridge, tea and coffee-making things and a television set, and at one end are two make-up chairs in front of big mirrors with lights around them.

We are taken back up onto the stage to see the set-up. It is the standard one of a compere's seat in the middle and an angled row of seats for the competitors on either side.

Helen, Mary and I try out our positions. The seats are just basic plastic chairs and the table in front of each team quite flimsy, just chipboard with light pine legs; it looks as if it would collapse if all three of us leaned on it at the one time. From what I had noticed by going with Nicholas to a couple of television studios in Brisbane, typical set quality.

All the other competitors arrive and we are introduced to them and to the compere, a local newsreader called Tim. We meet the adjudicator and his 'expert panel', who will sit at a table off to one side.

Stage lights come on and Margaret, who will direct the televising at seven, gives us the usual talk about acting natural and forgetting about the cameras. She says that she will use both afternoon quizzes as rehearsals for the evening production and that there could be a hold up now and then as she tries different camera angles; I wonder if part of the reason for that will be Mary's face.

'Big River' and 'Lowlands' are asked to take their places and 'Delta' and 'Redspear' are banished to our dressing room. There I switch on the monitor and we admire the transformation of the set. The props now look solid and permanent, and the colours that had seemed garish and uncoordinated now look tasteful under the television lights.

The curtain goes up and there's a storm of applause, even whistling. The competitors respond to their supporters with smiles and waves and the atmosphere lifts, as it does in our room.

***

The three Delta women are, I suppose, all in their fifties, grey haired or greying, medium to short in height – all on the plumpish side – and dressed for comfort rather than fashion; they speak of how overwhelming all this is. They start to unwrap cakes and slices that you know they themselves have cooked; one starts to make tea for all of us, and another begins to knit. It's true – they *are* unnerving.

I test myself against the questions being asked now on the stage and I suppose Mary and Helen are doing the same. The other three seem to take hardly any notice of the monitor, talking to each other and sometimes to one of us. At one point the knitter says, "do you mind?" and holds her creation up to my back. "My Reg is just your size." Helen catches my eye and grins.

I want to see what the show looks like from inside the hall and I excuse myself and walk up a side passage and open a door. The hall is full, probably eight hundred people. (I am used to estimating numbers for my Gazette reports so I am pretty confident about that.) As my eyes grow accustomed to the dark I see that there are people standing along the walls and at the back. A *very* full house.

The compere makes an effort at humour and raises a few laughs, but the Big River and Lowlands struggle is a bit dour – not much humour from those two teams of men. I resolve to try for some laughs when we are on. Big River gets 46.5 points and Lowlands 37.

***

I don't know whether Redspear gets a run of extra tough questions or whether we are just not thinking well, but we fall behind. In our rounds back home the questions, though addressed to individuals, were actually to the whole team, so that if, say, I did not know the answer to my question I could consult, and a correct answer still won the whole point. At this level though, if we have to confer, we get only half a point. At the halfway point we are down 25.5 to 29.

Grace has indeed continued to knit, like Madam Defarge at the guillotine in "A Tale of Two Cities". I had thought I could probably have some fun with that; she was sitting at the far end of her panel so I knew that the audience could see the knitting too. In fact the director threw that shot of her up onto the monitor every now and then.

I was thinking of calling foul – that she was destroying our concentration – that the clicking of the needles was putting us off – even that we were worried she might drop a stitch when her side was struggling for an answer. But they have not done any struggling, and it is Redspear that is on the back foot.

I feel I can't joke about the knitting while we are down – it might seem like whingeing – and meanwhile the Delta belles just keep smiling, and every row that goes onto those darn needles seems to put them further ahead.

They are distinctive in the way they answer. When a question comes to one of them she looks to the front while the other two turn and look at her, very still. Quite the opposite from our mob; we look anywhere but at the questionee. Helen often cups her head on her hands, leans on her elbows and stares straight ahead. She sometimes closes her eyes. Mary sits back and looks up at the ceiling or around the hall, as if she wishes she had something to read.

The Deltas on the other hand keenly watch the one under pressure. It's quite funny when it's the middle one and the others turn in on her. The questionee looks straight ahead then turns to the others and nods. They sit back, knitting recommences and the answer is given. Lots of smiles, and more nods. If she shakes her head they then confer – but there have been very few shakes.

I have to say they make me think of three Country Women's Association ladies deciding on the fruit cake entries at a show; I am sure they themselves make excellent fruit cakes. If the C.W.A. could nominate judges to the High Court the nominees would very likely look just like them.

While our side does get all our half points we are not getting enough of the whole ones. Helen and Mary are doing better than me. My strong suit is current affairs but there have not been many questions in that category and the general knowledge questions have found me wanting. I declare that it was Leonardo da Vinci who painted the ceiling of the Sistine Chapel.

I take some comfort from the fact that it is the two teams with the highest scores this afternoon that will meet for this evening's televised bout, and we are doing much better than either Lowlands or Big River.

We do begin to haul Delta in but they still beat us, 55 to 53.5.

***

We have an hour's break before the final and I propose a walk to Helen and Mary. Mollie has put the kettle on and looks genuinely disappointed when we say we'll pass.

"You don't mind do you?" I ask my partners when we are outside. "I had to get away for a bit."

"Oh me too," says Helen. "They're daunting."

Mary laughs, "Put the wind up us."

"Will we beat them?" I wonder.

"Every chance." Mary says. "But remind me to give you a talk on early Italian painters some time."

***

So we stroll the late Saturday afternoon streets of Manningham. Not as quiet as Redspear's streets at the same time, but this is a regional city, and lots of big stores are still open. The Learmonth Theatre is outside the CBD, but one can still hear a sort of big-town buzz. The street parking is full, but I suppose our show is part of the reason for that.

The cards fall our way that evening. Delta get three or four questions that none can answer individually and we get a nice run that we each get right. By half way we are four points ahead.

I feel brave enough now to try a funny line about the knitting and get chuckles from the women. When I try something similar a couple of minutes later the women slap each other's shoulders and Grace holds up her wool to the audience and makes an exaggerated knitting movement and gets a laugh. From then on it is a running joke; Grace holds the needles erect when they get a point, and the compere gets into the spirit too. "Delta Knit 36 Redspear Purl 39." That might not look so funny on paper but it is a riot this evening. And we win 57.5 to 52.

***

I admire our competitors. They have kept their good humour right to the end, smiling as if ten points *ahead*, and they seem downright happy with the result. While they make a final pot of tea in the dressing room and bring out yet more home-cooked delights, they bag each other and praise us.

When a husband arrives and says he's double parked they gather things briskly, say goodbye and bustle through the door. They've already told us they will compete next year.

As she reaches the door Grace brandishes her knitting bag at us; I fall back in dismay and she disappears chortling.

NINETEEN

THINGS HAPPENING

I thought – on our return from Manningham two weeks ago – that it was almost time to bring these scribblings to a close; one more story – about the Brisbane Final – would make a good ending, whether we won or not. You know my town now, and have met my friends – and have learned probably more than you really wanted to know about yours truly. Perhaps that shore for the Redspear 'river' was not far off.

***

Mary, Helen and I have, if I may say, good general knowledge, but it is very useful that each of us is stronger in certain areas. Mary is very good on the arts and Helen on history; if I have strengths they are in geography and current affairs, but I thought some study could only help, so I decided to retreat a little from the world, curb my curiosity about my friends and what they are up to, and spend more time reading.

But what did whatshisname say – 'life is what happens to you while you're busy making other plans'; Helen calls Mary and me to her motel to tell us she has decided to quit the team.

"I don't mean 'quit'. I mean *step aside* – for Robbie."

"But the television people..." says Mary. "We signed a contract."

"And we shouldn't have. So what if Robbie's in a wheelchair? Let's tell them to get over it!"

"Helen, it's more – well – his face..." but as I say that I hear how weak it sounds.

"It's not perfect. So what!?"

Mary shuffles. "We know *I* have the face that worries them more. I think it's the thought of *two* of us up there ..."

"Yes – and I'm 'presentable' – but no, Mary, it's not right. Those attitudes should be dead and buried. We shouldn't pander to them. I won't."

Mary nods; she is accepting this.

"There's this legal obligation though," I repeat, but Mary now has a look that I have seen before; decision made.

"Ring them Hugh. Tell them we *will* have Robbie back in."

***

I do as I am told, that night, and from home. There is a long silence from Grainger, then a sigh; had he been expecting this?

"Hugh, you know there is this contract. I'd have to get this past our legal people. Could be tricky." Pause. "I understood that you were a bit unhappy about our insistence that Helen Carruthers stay in your team, but we did put up that extra sponsorship for you."

"Yes, and thanks again for that. But, well – Mary and I were living with the other thing but Helen feels she can't."

"And she....."

"*Won't* go on."

Another silence. I can imagine a pen being fiddled with, and a chair being tilted back. Then, "I understand this illness of Helen's is quite serious Hugh?"

"Er..." I catch on. "Yes. Not life threatening but..."

"A virus you said? The doctor recommending no travel?"

"Exactly."

"And in case our legal people get sticky, a doctor's certificate would be available?"

Old McGauran would do it. "Of course."

A chuckle from the other end. "Well that's that then. Any other problems Hugh?"

I think a bottle of good whisky is the least the man deserves.

***

When I tell Helen on the phone I half expect some criticism about the sickness ruse – we are in the realm of *principle* here. There is a pause but then a giggle.

"Well, I think I *am* coming down with something. How observant of you."

I phone Mary and she says she will tell Robbie. Rob!

***

I ring her again late in the day. "How did he take it?"

"As matter of factly as before. Just said 'righto'."

***

One morning Rob turns up at my house in a red two door Mercedes coupé. He insists on taking me for a drive; we head up the highway to the north. I'm afraid the state's speed limits are well and truly ignored.

145

At the turnoff to the Booroon mine we turn around and begin to tool back to town at a sedate hundred. He tells me that he had seen the car advertised in Brisbane's "Courier Mail" a couple of weeks before; he rang the dealers, who trucked it up to their branch in Manningham. One of their people had driven it out from there for Rob to try. They would keep it in Manningham if Rob did not buy it.

It did cross my mind that it was somewhat odd that a 'disabled' man should have a car like this but then I asked myself why? Because this is a glamour car and he is not glamorous? Because I had not imagined Rob behind the wheel of anything less conservative than his green Volvo? Which, I suppose, must be at least ten years old. A new car was due, and why shouldn't this rich young man have something flash?

"Surprised?"

"Yes – but it's a beauty. I'm envious. I want to drive it sometime."

He laughs. "Okay. When we come back from Brisbane. I'll take Mary down in it."

***

"Will I be safe?" asks Mary.

"Of course." I've told her about our morning gallop. "He's a good driver, you know that."

"Yes. Ordinarily. But *this* machine. Talk about Toad of Toad Hall! Do you know I saw him go out three times from the office yesterday and fondle the thing." We both laugh – but I was the same in my younger days. Two Toads.

"Another thing. Today in the office there are two new catalogues on men's clothes. I've always felt he didn't much care what he wore. Something's happening." She gives me a keen look. "Do you know anything?"

146

"No." I hadn't mentioned to Mary Robbie's reference to the jet plane; he would choose the time to talk to her. And then because I know how her mind runs, "I don't know of any woman either."

She does not like being in the dark, but she shrugs and changes the subject. "Now – my will."

My shoulders metaphorically sag; what this time I wonder? If she has decided to make changes, this will make it four times in as many years. Rob and I are her executors, and though she doesn't *have* to tell us why she wants a change, she does.

***

About five years ago she lost both former executors. Hinton, her solicitor, a man twenty years her junior, died of a heart attack, then Mavis Earnshaw, an old friend – a widow – married a man from New South Wales and moved south. Rob and I were dragooned.

Having no dependants, Mary had decided years before to leave her wealth to people who could do some good with it. Her first will listed orphanages, charities, churches and aid organisations.

The first change was brought on by revelations about abuse in Catholic orphanages and 'homes'. "It's dreadful Hugh, and the Cardinals and the Archbishops are acting as if it didn't happen. It's probably *still* happening!" They got the chop.

Then there was the inquiry which showed fraud in two big aid organisations including one listed in the will. Out it went: more money for the rest.

A journalist did a detailed piece about the Anglican dioceses in Sydney and Brisbane which she read as evidence they were pushing people out of their properties so that they could redevelop them. They were gone – the last of the churches, except for the Salvation Army, which I think she regards more as a charity.

As it stands the current beneficiaries are charities – local, state and national – with Rob and I having the prerogative to add others if we see fit. Her estate is to be disbursed annually, in roughly equal instalments, and over ten years.

***

I groan – quietly – and get a look, but as she shifts in her chair – 'settling' I would call the movement – I get the impression once again that *she* enjoys these changes.

"I have decided I want my money to be used directly to help children."

"Yes? In what way?"

"I want the money to provide equality of opportunity."

"Like a Benefit Fund?"

"Yes."

"That's what some of these charities do now."

"No they don't. They give food and clothing and blankets."

"And some help kids."

"Yes, yes, some do." She swivels in her chair, energetic. "I know that's important Hugh and I'm still going to support that. You'll have heaps for that." 'Heaps' is right – many tens of millions of dollars. "I'm thinking of what that politician said about no child living in poverty. I don't want a child in this town, in this district anywhere around here," waving an arm, "living in *mental* poverty." She takes a breath and then delivers a line that I think she may have rehearsed. "Not able to achieve its potential, and living to regret it."

We talk about it for a while, but I realise we will need Rob there sometime for a much longer talk. One thing I do grasp is that what she is proposing could occupy a great deal of my time, and for the rest of my life. I am not sure if she appreciates this but I do not mention it now.

***

Once again I try to concentrate on some study but I cannot step out of our town's life entirely. On Saturday night there is our big Winter Ball in the Civic Centre, and my family has booked a table. There's always a theme for the ball and this year it is "Fred and Ginger".

We men have to wear formal wear, dinner suits or tuxedos at the least and tail coats if we can manage. There are some imaginative attempts; the men from "Osmond" get a round of applause when they all appear with silver tail coats. These prove to be urea bags turned inside out and sewn together. They begin to fall apart through the evening but for a while they look pretty smart.

The women, of course, have really got into it. Those slim enough to manage it are wearing tight dresses with floor length flowing hems. Stouter types have wisely gone instead for effect with hair styles, makeup and big corsages. There are at least a dozen Ginger Rogers look-alikes. Evita McAdam has come as Carmen Miranda, complete with a towering headdress of flowers and fruit.

Helen Carruthers' distant cousin Michael has made it to Redspear in time for the event. (I forgot to mention that we met him in Manningham and he celebrated with us that night after the quiz.) It is only after I recognise *him* tonight that I realise that his 'Ginger' is our Helen.

The tables have been grouped around the edges of the dance floor and decorated to look like those nightclub tables of the 30's and 40's that seemed to feature in all F and G's movies. It has been cleverly done; batteries have been used for the little table lights.

I share a table with my son Ralph and his wife Sally and Sally's friend and her husband who are up from New South Wales. Helen and Michael are at a table just across the floor from ours and I notice that they seem to be engrossed in each other. I know that if Mary were here she would be very interested in seeing that. (She had decided not to come; "those big crowded dances are not for me anymore".)

***

I meet Helen at the post office on the Monday and compliment her on her Ginger.

"It's been a nice weekend." Then a whoop of laughter. "She was on the phone this morning. Wanting to know *everything*."

"I'll bet. I know I'll have a devil of a time too if I ever..." She tilts her head, amusement in those remarkable eyes.

"If you ever ...?"

I take a breath and a chance. "Begin a relationship."

"Is that what I've done?"

"Look, I don't want to know. I'm sorry."

Her good mood is unbreakable. "Well I don't know about a 'relationship' but we do enjoy each other's company."

***

One morning I phone my daughter Julie to check if I can have a bed on my way to the Final in Brisbane. Her property is about halfway, right on the highway. I say "hers" but I suppose it is still owned by her parents-in-law; Peter's mother and father are retired in Toowoomba now.

Pete answers. "No need to ring Hugh, you know you can always just turn up." He is a no frills, solid young man; Julie chose a good one.

I phone Nicholas in Brisbane and get Messagebank. Around midday, Haydon returns the call; he has spoken with Nick and it's 'cool'.

"Will you be there Haydon?"

"Yes."

150

"We'll cook up something special." Haydon and I both like cooking. "How about a fish curry. Thai?"

He says something that sounds like 'dee mar'. "That's 'good' in Thai." A pause. "It will be a farewell dinner Mr. Watson."

"Oh?"

"I am moving into my own flat." Another pause. "Kirsten – do you know her?" and then before I can answer, "hasn't Nick said anything ... ?"

"No." I had met this Kirsten a couple of times – short, dark haired, energetic, quick moving and quick talking; I remember thinking 'so different to Nick'. "She'll be moving in?"

"Yes."

"So – they're ...?"

"Yes."

I take a moment. "Well there you go. Fathers are the last to know these things. When?"

"In about two weeks. She's holidaying in New Zealand at the moment."

After I hang up I reflect that Haydon sounded flat. I have the thought that he would probably have liked to stay with Nick.

***

It is now only a few days from the Brisbane Final but I *have* studied diligently. I have listened to the news and the ABC's "A.M." and have watched the television current affairs programs and have read each day's "Australian" from front to back.

I have even browsed my atlas; I have noticed the quiz seems to feature "name two major rivers that rise in Tibet" type questions. Also, because the question setters often display a parochial bias, I have re-read Fitzgerald's "History of Queensland". I do not know how much the others have done – little, I suspect – but perhaps they have less need.

***

Just two days before we are due to leave, Rob invites himself around for a drink after work. He makes his way on his sticks from his new car to the verandah and tells me something for which I am quite unprepared. He intends to purchase sex.

"I've never even got close to a sexual relationship with anyone. I don't meet many young women and those I have met don't look twice."

"They don't even look once. Properly."

He shrugs. "Their loss. I think I'd be pretty good in bed. But I'm going to give it a go Hugh. Got to. If I have to buy it, so be it."

"It – won't be the same."

"As 'lurrve'?" He is grinning but blushing now too. "Yeah I know, but it'll have to do in the meantime. But hey, I'm in unknown territory here. Do you look up the 'Yellow Pages' in Brisbane or something?"

"Well – I know the girls do advertise there. And in the "Courier Mail". 'Escorts' they call themselves."

"And they come to your hotel?"

"Yes – or sometimes you can go to them."

"I think I'd rather someone come to me."

"I'll be in Brisbane before you," I find myself saying. "Would you like me to – ring a few? Do some research?"

"Great. You don't mind?"

I spread my hands in a stage Jewish gesture. "My boy, I'm an agent remember."

I make us a drink, and we go to my favourite spot on the verandah, that north-east corner with the little table and the two squatter chairs. I try to give the impression I am treating his news lightly, but I know I shall be thinking about it later. It's a big step – and yet not I suppose such a big one; I know that millions of young men have had their first sexual adventure with 'professionals' – but this is different. Rob is a mature, educated and in many respects experienced man, but he has been more of a son to me than just a friend. Family.

***

Now – the last and most dramatic interruption to my studies – the probable solving of our graffiti mystery. Georgia bustles into my office at the agency.

"Do you have five minutes?" She almost frogmarches me to her car.

"What is it?"

"That toilet stuff." It is weeks since the last one; surely it hasn't started again! We head down the street. "Do you know who it is?" I get a sideways look, but that's all. She's enjoying this.

Inside the police station she parks me in front of a board of notices and memos. Obediently I look from one to the other, and as I work my way along them Georgia practically writhes beside me.

I come to one that sets out a roster for weekend duty, typed. Whoever has put the sheet there has pinned it on top of another which is longer. One can read some of the words on it; they are handwritten, and in a very distinctive style.

"It's identical," she says. It looks that way to me too. I ask Constable Damian, who is on duty, to look at it.

"Who would have written that?"

"Sergeant Hagan."

"Are you sure?"

"Pretty sure. See that date. That's in his time, and he used to make up all the rosters."

"Do you have any other things written by him?"

"Oh yes. All his notes." He stops and stands now, four square, the young law man on duty. "What's up?"

"I'm just having a bet with Georgia." I'm not ready yet to crucify the sergeant. I smile. "Would you mind if we had a look?"

Damian brings one of Hagan's reports – *and it is not in the same handwriting*. Georgia and I both show puzzlement and Damian takes it over to the noticeboard to compare.

"It's different," he says, and then "oh, I know, *Mrs.* Hagan used to write up some of these."

***

Back at my home I make myself a coffee and try to make sense of this. If it was Deborah Hagan who wrote those messages was it because she knew or guessed her husband had a crush on Helen?

But then – driving all those kilometres to write at the Rest Areas – undetected? Possible I suppose – she had her own car, and her husband wouldn't necessarily have known where she went during the day.

And finally – shooting at her husband!?

Hot stuff for Redspear.

TWENTY

THE FINAL

It's a Friday morning and I have been in Brisbane since the previous evening, staying at Nick's apartment. The Final will be tomorrow night at eight, in the television studios – to be broadcast live – and I am looking forward to it.

***

Rob left home with Mary yesterday morning too but much later than I, and they stopped on the way, as I guessed they would. They should be in Brisbane by midday today. Mary will stay at the old Park Hotel, near the Botanic Gardens, where she always stays. She takes a suite they call the MacArthur, named after the general, and Rob has booked a room at the Sheraton; I shall go and see him there after he arrives.

I do not have great news for him. I tried several Escort ads last night and spoke to four women in all. They sounded alright, and they were all relaxed about visiting a man who is physically handicapped, but when I asked them to describe themselves their game dropped. Out came the clichés – model looks, wild tumbled hair, spectacular breasts, tiny waists, taut bodies – and it was all unbelievable.

With the fourth woman I actually laughed at some description. I felt forced to explain my lapse of manners and as we talked things changed. "Exotic Ninette" began to disappear and Sharon, a suburban Brisbane girl, began to emerge. We had a long chat. She told me she had left home at fifteen to get away from her mother's defacto. She'd become a street kid and got into drugs and then into 'escorting' to pay for her habit. She said she had been off drugs for two years and had a nice place and reckoned she now had a pretty good life. She said she was twenty-two.

I told her I would recommend her to Rob – and I will – but I find my heart is not in this. And you know me well enough to know it is not prudery; I'm relaxed about what consenting adults do. Prostitution though – there can be a victim there. And again – well – it's *Robbie*.

***

I had waited till Nick went out last night before making the calls from his lounge room, but Haydon returned to the apartment while I was still talking with Sharon. He motioned that he would leave me alone, but I signed it was okay; he sat down with a glass of wine on the lounge. I caught his eye while asking a fairly explicit question and he raised his eyebrows and made to get up again, but I waved him back. From then he listened with frank interest; when I finished I told him about Rob.

Haydon told me that he was still looking for his own place. He wanted a flat close to the city but smaller and cheaper than Nick's; he would be living on his own.

"I think that will suit me for a while."

"No bed for a country visitor?"

"You'd always be welcome Mr. Watson."

***

At three in the afternoon Mary rings me on my mobile and I go to see her at the Park. There is a framed photo and a plaque just inside the door to remind us of the room's earlier distinguished occupant. The view over the Botanic Gardens from the cane chairs on the balcony is very nice. Very expensive too, I would think.

"A good trip?"

"It wasn't bad. You can put the passenger seat right back. I slept most of the way."

"So Rob's driving didn't worry you?"

"No," she laughs. "I think he must have already got most of 'Toad' out of his system. You know he's been taking drives everywhere the last two weeks."

She says they could have made Brisbane by eight last night but she had begged off at a town about three hours out. "There's a nice motel there – I've stayed before. Rob didn't mind too much, though he did seem very keen to get here."

Rob had phoned me from his room at that motel late at night. I had told him about my 'research' and given him Sharon's number.

"Rob's at the Sheraton. I suppose you know. I wanted him to try this place." I understand why he would want to be somewhere else; Mary could easily get it into her head to visit his room.

***

I go now to see Rob at the Sheraton. "Did you ring Sharon?"

"Yes. We talked quite a while."

"And ...?"

"She'll come here at nine o'clock" I accept the offer of an orange juice from his bar fridge. "You look a bit worried."

"Well – I feel a bit responsible. And I've never seen this girl."

"How do you think I feel? She's never seen *me*."

"Did you describe yourself?"

157

"Didn't need to. She repeated what you told her. Pretty accurate; I corrected it a little."

"On what?"

"Well – she had me down as Mr. Universe."

"You are very strong."

"Yes, well, I toned that down a bit. But you know, I don't think she's worried about all this." He gestures at the wheelchair.

"No, I agree."

"So – tonight's the night." We toast the occasion. "Have a last look at 'Rob the Virgin'."

***

There is a reception at the television studios in the late afternoon. Our opponents are to be the Darling Downs team again, with the same members as last year, and we greet each other like old friends. Friendly enemies; they are formidable, and last year held us to a draw.

The manager gives us a tour of the building; in one control room a panel program is being taped. The director is a young woman, possibly in her late twenties, and after the taping she chats with us; we have lots of questions and she handles them all well.

***

Sex. Or love. Both. They drive the world for sure and if I needed reminders I've just had another.

Back at Nick's flat for the night, and making an omelette from bits and pieces from his fridge, I offered to expand the finished product for Haydon when he came in after work. His greeting was friendly as usual but he sounded tired; he had a shower while I cooked and made up a salad. I opened a bottle of Sauvignon Blanc.

***

I knew that Haydon had a job in computer graphics and that he often worked long hours. What did he do for a social life? He never seemed to stay away overnight, at least while I was there, and whenever I phoned at night from Redspear it was often he who answered then too.

I can be as blinkered as the next person, and so I was proving to be. I said something about it being nice of him to spend time with an oldie when he could be out with friends of his own age; he laid his knife and fork down and looked at me.

"I love your son Mr. Watson."

Just why this had not occurred to me I have no idea, but of course it made sense as soon as he said it. Not *as soon* because I still had to scrabble over my personal hurdle of hearing a man say he loved another man. *That* way. But yes – it all clicked.

He said that he had finally told Nick just a few weeks before.

"What did Nick say?"

"Not much. What could he say? I got a hug. And a kiss on the forehead. First and last."

He smiled but it was half-hearted. He affected an older "that's life" air, but if anything he looked even younger. Though I could not identify with his sexual preferences, I felt sympathy for him.

We tidied up in the kitchen, and as Haydon put glasses and dishes away I felt there was a drained air to his movements. He caught me looking at him and gave a half smile and a sigh and lifted and dropped his shoulders. I walked over and hugged him and he dropped his head onto my shoulder.

***

I went to bed at ten but was not tired; I kept the light on and read – "Cloud Street". Haydon went past the open door on the way from his bedroom to the kitchen and on his way back he stopped for a word. It is a double bed and I moved over and folded back the sheet and blanket. Haydon smiled and got in but very soon was asleep. I was still not tired, and kept reading.

***

At eleven the phone rings and it is Rob. He had cancelled the visit from Sharon.

"I just thought I'd give it a bit longer. You know, I think I'm just getting my act together."

"I think that's a good idea."

"Do you? I can tell you it is hard. Double entendre intended." A laugh. "I am glad we don't yet have those vision phones."

So, at the moment – I think – am I.

***

We win the final, quite comfortably as it turns out, with Mary and Rob at their knowledgeable best; the station people do not fuss at all at having to deal with two 'physically challenged' participants.

Grainger has come down from the regional office at Manningham for the night; I suspect he has done some spade work, and if so this is a triumph for him. Both the general manager of the network *and* the chairman are there, and they put on a little party for us. They are particularly friendly: the chairman says "it takes something like this to change people's attitudes, *thank you*," and shakes my hand earnestly, and I do wonder if they know that Helen's illness is bogus. Well, I think, perhaps we have done some good; I decide to make it *two* bottles of whisky for Grainger.

Something even better happens. The director of the production has been the young woman we met in the studios the day before. At the party she is warm and relaxed. Attractive – and I am not the only one to think so; Rob takes the plunge and asks her out. He has told me he will stay in Brisbane for a while.

***

So now I am driving back to Redspear, the old girl slumbering in the passenger seat beside me. She said she is delighted for Rob; she has he and Roseanne married already. Well, whatever happens there, I think Rob has 'moved on'.

Mary also has Helen married to her cousin Michael, the engineer who lives and works on the coast, and who has visited Redspear twice since Manningham. If they do marry, or become 'partners', will they live in Redspear? They could continue to live more or less as they do now, and commute, but I wonder how long they could keep that up. Would Helen depart? Is another of my friends about to move on?

If Rob does leave Redspear, Mary will need to find a new manager. But perhaps this remarkable woman, now in her late eighties, will decide to retire. Or is it the need to stay abreast of her business interests that helps to keep her mind so sharp? Whichever way it goes, she will grow I am sure ever more wealthy – will change her will again – and remain as energetically curious about the affairs of her friends as ever.

And I...? Well, I shall continue to live in Redspear. Some might regard this town as isolated – something of a backwater – but home as they say is what you make it. *I* certainly do not feel as if I am out of touch with the world – do not feel as if things are passing me by. And there will always be a drink and some food on that verandah, for old friends and new.

THE WRITER

Ron Iddon is probably best known in Australia for his work on the ABC's long running television series "A BIG COUNTRY", as reporter and director.

He left the ABC to become an independent filmmaker, eventually writing and directing twenty more documentaries, all of which were shown on television; "Peppimenarti", about life in an Aboriginal settlement in the Northern Territory, was nominated for 'Best Documentary' in the AFI Awards.

By the mid-1980's he had three co-written non-fiction books to his credit and for the past ten years he has been writing fiction. In late 2011 he released "The Short Stories of Ron Iddon-The Murray River Collection" and in mid- 2012 "The Short Stories of Ron Iddon-The Queensland Collection".

Ron lives in Toowoomba, southern Queensland. He writes every day, and is also a part-time teacher in literacy; his recreation is the study and restoration of antique Australian furniture. (More on his web site, *roniddon.com.au*)

EARLIER BOOKS BY THIS AUTHOR

NON-FICTION

(In collaboration)

A Big Country (John Mabey)

A Big Country (John Mabey)

The Stockman (Mary Durack, R.M.Williams et al)

FICTION

(Solo)

The Short Stories of Ron Iddon-The Murray River Collection

The Short stories of Ron Iddon- The Queensland Collection

Both collections of short stories, and this book, are available only on
the internet, via www. roniddon.com.au
or www.leopardwoodproductions.com.au

 **LEOPARDWOOD
PRODUCTIONS**

www.ingramcontent.com/pod-product-compliance
Lightning Source LLC
Chambersburg PA
CBHW060402030726
47497CB00003B/817